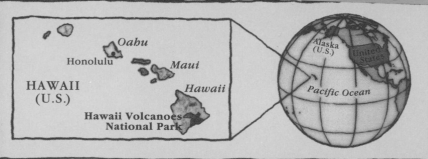

Oahu

Honolulu

Maui

HAWAII
(U.S.)

Hawaii

Hawaii Volcanoes
National Park

Alaska
(U.S.)

United
States

Pacific Ocean

(11)

Glenwood

Volcano
House

Kilauea Visitor Center

Volcano Village

Kilauea Iki Crater

Thurston Lava Tube

*Kilauea
Caldera*

Jaggar
Museum

EAST RIFT ZONE

Puu Oo

*Puu
Puai*

Devastation
Trail

Puu Huluhulu

*Halemaumau
Crater*

Mauna Ulu

CHAIN OF CRATERS ROAD

PACIFIC OCEAN

HAWAII VOLCANOES NATIONAL PARK

National Parks
Mystery #2

RAGE OF
FIRE

GLORIA SKURZYNSKI AND ALANE FERGUSON

National Geographic Society
Washington, D.C.

Note: The Hawaiian language uses such special marks as glottal stops (') and macrons (‾). In *Rage of Fire*, we have followed the style set by the National Geographic Society's cartographers, using these marks for all Hawaiian words except place names. If written with marks, the word Halemaumau, for example, would appear as Halema'uma'u (pronounced Ha-leh-mah-oo-mah-oo).

Text copyright © 1998
Gloria Skurzynski and Alane Ferguson

Endpaper map by Matthew Frey—Wood Ronsaville Harlin, Inc.
We appreciate the assistance of Carl Mehler, NGS Senior Map Editor.
Photo insert credits: Kona coast, Robert Madden, NGS;
Sea turtle, Bates Littlehales; Nēnē, Chris Johns, NGP;
'Ōhelo berries, Steve Raymer; Kilauea Iki Crater, William H. Amos;
Puu Oo volcano, James Amos.

Photo insert and map ©1998 National Geographic Society

This is a work of fiction. Any resemblance to living persons or events other than descriptions of natural phenomena is purely coincidental.

Library of Congress Cataloging-in-Publication Data
Skurzynski, Gloria
    Rage of Fire / Gloria Skurzynski and Alane Ferguson
    p. cm. (National parks mystery ; #2)
    Summary: Jack, Ashley, and their parents visit Hawaii where
they meet a Vietnamese boy who is going to live with his
American grandfather whom he has never met, and are pursued
by the Goddess Pele.
    ISBN 0-7922-7035-5
    1. Hawaii—Juvenile fiction. [1. Hawaii—Fiction.
2. Pele (Hawaiian deity)—Fiction. 3. Vietnamese Americans—
Fiction. 4. Mystery and detective stories.]
    I. Ferguson, Alane. II. Title III. Series.
PZ7.S6287Rag 1998   97-41125
[Fic]—dc21   CIP

Printed in the United States of America

ACKNOWLEDGMENTS

The authors are extremely grateful to
Darcy Hu, wildlife biologist;
Bobby Camara, cave specialist;
and Mardie Lane, public information officer,
all of Hawaii Volcanoes National Park.

For Ed Skurzynski,
who makes all things possible,
with love from his wife and his daughter.

*N*one *of them saw her, of that she was sure. Heads bobbing like nēnē, they argued among themselves. As she watched the girl and the two boys, she knew a truth as surely as she knew the spirit of the volcano: these children did not fear the wrath of Pele.*

And for that there was a price.

Lightning slashed the heavens as she raised her arms. "Hea? Ka mea hea? *Which of you is the one?*"

The children turned and saw her, their eyes widening in sudden fear.

"Hea? Ka mea hea?" *she screamed again, but her words were drowned in a burst of thunder.*

Now the children scattered from her, past the bones of trees littering the trail.

She would find them. They must not get away.

They looked like long blue pencils, shiny and slick. Swarms of them swam around Jack's head, so close he thought they might bump into his face. Each time he reached out to touch one of them, the whole fleet of silver-blue needlefish darted just beyond his fingertips. They were as impossible to grasp as liquid mercury.

Cool! he thought, but he couldn't say it because his face was underwater. Snorkeling in the Hawaiian waters was a lot easier than he'd expected. The hardest part had been putting on the fins and waddling out into the ocean: Those long, floppy flippers on his feet made him stagger like a flustered duck. Once he got past the jagged volcanic rocks on the shoreline to where he could bellyflop into the waves, everything was easier. Hanging just under the surface of the ocean, breathing rhythmically through his snorkel, Jack could look at endless varieties of rainbow-colored fish as they glided silently beneath him. And below the fish, on the very bottom of the ocean floor, lay the coral reefs.

His dad had told him not to step on the coral, because the reefs were made up of tiny living organisms, and any weight on them would damage them. But after an hour of fish watching, Jack's face mask was getting cloudy. He needed a place to stand so he could take off the mask and wipe out the fog.

He saw a big rock beneath him. Perfect. It would be a good place to get his bearings, too. Swimming head down, staring into the clear water, made it dangerously easy to lose his sense of direction and go too far out, where he might get caught in a Pacific Ocean current.

Balancing on the rock, Jack took off his mask and let the snorkel dangle from its strap. The beach didn't look too far away. He could see his mother stretched out on a beach chair, getting tan. Olivia Landon never burned like Jack and his dad did, so she could lie in the warm sun and turn golden. Still, she'd painted her nose white with zinc sunscreen, just in case. A magazine sat spine up like a pup tent on her stomach as she dozed. Good, Jack thought, maybe sun and sleep would melt off some of her stress. A long winter tending animals had left her more tired than usual. If she got really rested, Jack mused, he might be able to talk her into a new camera lens he'd been longing for. Rest, Mom, rest, he silently commanded.

Suddenly, about a hundred feet from Jack, Ashley started to scream. "Mom, hurry, you've got to come! Quick!"

Her arms flailed on the surface of the waves and she bobbed up and down, looking like she was sinking. Skinny, almost-11-year-old Ashley had no body fat to keep her afloat. Her head dipped under the waves for an instant until she flipped herself back up and cried out again.

"Hurry!" she screamed. "Jack, Mom! Over here!"

Ashley was in trouble! Jack had been told to keep an eye on his younger sister and make sure they stayed close together while they swam, but since he'd begun watching the fish, he hadn't paid much attention to Ashley. Quickly, he slid his face mask back on, clamped the snorkel's mouthpiece between his lips, and beat the water with his arms and legs as hard as he could.

Worried that he couldn't get to her fast enough, he kept rearing up his head to see if his mother had heard Ashley's screams.

Olivia leapt out of the beach chair and took off running over the sharp volcanic rocks as if they were smooth sand. She made a flat dive into the surf and swam furiously toward Ashley.

Both Jack and Olivia reached her at the same time.

"Put your arm around my neck," Olivia panted. "Don't worry. You're safe."

Jack yanked the snorkel out of his mouth. "You'll be OK now," he gasped, treading water and trying to catch his breath. "We'll get you back to shore."

"No. I'm fine."

"You're fine!" Jack sputtered. "I thought—"

"I just saw a sea turtle. It was *huge!* Maybe three feet long! You gotta see it!"

"What!" Olivia cried. "You made all that fuss over a turtle!"

Ashley bobbed in the waves, getting a mouthful of seawater and spitting it out. "Yeah! Turtles are rare. We gotta look for it before it gets away."

Now it was Olivia who sputtered. "You scared me half to death! Don't ever, ever yell like that again unless you're in real trouble."

"I'm sorry, Mom." Remorse skimmed across Ashley's face, but only for an instant. Just long enough, Jack imagined, for her to assure herself of their mother's automatic pardon: "Honestly, Ashley, you about gave me a heart attack."

"Since you're already out here, Mom, don't you want to see the turtle? I promise, he was right under my feet."

"No, I'm going back to shore." Trying to stay afloat in front of them, 50 feet offshore with no swim fins or snorkel gear, Olivia had to tread water without stopping. It was too deep for her to stand: Unlike their father, their mother wasn't very tall. "That turtle's probably halfway to Maui by now," she said. "You two keep close to each other, and don't try following it out to sea. I've had enough excitement without either of you getting dragged off in a rip current. Understand?" She pushed the wet hair out of her eyes to look first at Jack, then at Ashley.

"OK, Mom," Ashley answered meekly.

Shaking her head, Olivia added, "Our first full day in Hawaii. What a way to start." She swam away from them then. Olivia was a polished swimmer, able to glide along the ocean's surface as gracefully as the fish slid beneath it.

"Way to go, Ashley," Jack told her, splashing a handful of water at her face. "Mom's supposed to be taking it easy."

"But I saw a turtle!"

"You probably saw a clump of seaweed. Sea turtles don't come swimming around where people are." The most Jack and Ashley could expect to see, so close to the coastline, were the schools of brightly colored fish—and that was great all by itself. Fitting the mouthpiece against his teeth and pulling his mask over his eyes and nose, Jack again ducked his head beneath the waves.

A large, dark, shape slid through the water not five feet ahead of him, its front flippers waving like angel wings.

Jack threw up his head, spit out the snorkel, and yelled, "Ashley! A turtle!"

This Hawaiian vacation had been a surprise treat for the Landons. Olivia Landon, a wildlife veterinarian, sometimes got invited to consult on wildlife problems in America's national parks. Just a few weeks earlier, she'd had a phone call from Hawaii Volcanoes National Park on the largest of the Hawaiian Islands.

"Kids! You're not going to believe this!" she'd said that evening, coming into the kitchen with the portable phone still in her hand. "I mean, I think it's going to work out. What dates are your schools' spring breaks?"

"Next to last week in March," Jack had answered. In Jackson Hole, Wyoming, where the Landons lived, schools closed for a whole week each spring.

"Well," Olivia had begun, almost bouncing in excitement, "it just so happens I got a conservation grant to go to Hawaii Volcanoes National Park for a meeting, right in that exact week. The grant will pay all my expenses, including airfare."

"And you guys have that whole week off?"

their father, Steven, had broken in. "It might be possible—"

"Could we—?" Olivia asked.

"Take the whole family to Hawaii on vacation!" Ashley cried, jumping up. "Can we, Dad? Mom? Please, please, please!"

"Well, can we? I mean, afford it?" Jack had asked.

They'd all decided that with careful penny-pinching, they'd be able to manage. Not only could, but should, since their mother really needed a vacation. In the winter, Olivia worked at the National Elk Refuge in Jackson Hole. Thousands of elk migrated from Yellowstone National Park and other areas into the refuge, to be fed while the winter snows piled up too deep for them to forage. During those freezing months, Olivia labored hard and long to keep the elk herds alive, bringing sleds full of hay and animal feed to them all day every day, in below-zero temperatures, and frequently checking their physical conditions.

By March, those elk that survived—and most of them did—would begin to migrate north again, back into Yellowstone, where in May they'd give birth to their new calves.

"I'd love to have a really good rest on some nice, warm sand," Olivia had told them that evening in Jackson Hole, right after the phone call came. "This is going to be perfect."

And it had been. Now, at nine in the morning, on the day after the turtle sighting, the Landons were lounging on the balcony of their third-floor condo. Mango and papaya rinds mingled with crumpled napkins and empty cups on the glass-topped table. The Sunday newspaper had been dropped helter-skelter on the floor.

Warm air caressed their faces, while the gentle sun seemed to kiss their skin.

"I love being lazy," Olivia murmured.

"That's nice, Mom, but I want to go snorkeling again," Ashley announced. "It's awesome. How soon can we go today?"

"Dad, can I rent a boogie board?" Jack chimed in. "I saw these guys surfing with them, and they looked fun. Or maybe we could go scuba diving. There was a sign for lessons over at—"

"Take it easy, kids," Steven told them. "Your mother needs to relax. However...." He cleared his throat. "I wouldn't mind an early start on the whale watching. I lugged my heaviest long-distance lens all the way from Wyoming to get some good shots. Are you interested in whale watching with me, Olivia?"

Olivia groaned. "You're all ganging up on me. You're too ambitious. I want to relax today, and sit by the shore without anyone around—"

Just then the phone rang.

Steven looked at Ashley and Jack. "Who on earth could that be? Who even knows we're here?" Their mother climbed out of the deck chair and picked up the phone from an end table in the condo's living room. They'd been lucky to rent a two-bedroom condo, with a dining area and kitchen, for a reasonable price. That meant they could cook their own meals and save money on restaurants.

From the condo's balcony, Steven, Ashley, and Jack looked straight out at the Pacific, all the way to the horizon. Surfers were out, riding the waves. Jack wished his mother would hurry and get off the phone. He didn't want to waste a single minute of this beautiful Sunday.

Five minutes later, when Olivia returned, Steven asked, "Was it Hawaii Volcanoes National Park?"

"No." Her expression was strange.

"What, then? Problems at the elk refuge?"

She shook her head.

Sitting down on the deck chair, Olivia leaned her elbows on the glass-topped round table. "I—I don't know. I hope I did the right thing. It's just..."

"What, Mom?" Jack asked. "What'd you do?"

"I'm sorry. I just committed our whole family and I didn't even talk it over with any of you. It just seemed like...the right thing."

Ashley's brown eyes widened. "What is it? Another foster kid?"

Half a year earlier, the Landons had decided, as a family, to offer their home to kids needing temporary emergency care. Most of them stayed for not much more than a week, until permanent care could be arranged for them.

"Sort of. Not quite," Olivia answered. "But it's going to change our vacation plans."

"So tell us," Jack urged. "What's happening?"

"The call was from Social Services in Wyoming. It's an interesting case. There's a boy who's been living here in Hawaii. He's Vietnamese. His mother died a couple of years ago, and no one knows what happened to his father, so he was sent here to live with elderly relatives on the eastern side of the island. Close to Hawaii Volcanoes National Park."

"What does that have to do with any of us?" Steven asked.

"Well, the boy's great-aunt has serious health problems, and the great-uncle says they can't keep Danny anymore."

"Danny? Danny what?" Ashley wanted to know.

"His name is Danny Tran. He's nine years old."

"I still don't get it. Is he supposed to be our new foster kid?" Jack asked.

"No." Olivia took a deep breath. "Danny has

an American grandfather, a former soldier who served in Vietnam during the war. He lives in our city—in Jackson Hole. The grandfather just found out about Danny—before now he never even knew the boy existed. But he's willing to keep him permanently. If we can bring Danny back to Jackson Hole with us, the grandfather will take over Danny's care. I said we'd do it."

Steven looked perplexed. "Wait a minute. This vacation was supposed to give you some peace from a hard winter, Olivia. Taking on a strange kid isn't going to be exactly restful."

She shrugged and said, "You're right, but what could I tell them? The woman from Social Services knew we were over here; I'd mentioned our vacation when I spoke to her last week."

"But, the expense—"

"All Danny's expenses will be paid by his grandfather. Social Services will arrange the boy's flight reservations, so all we have to do is pick him up and bring him back to Wyoming." Olivia paused, and asked again, "What else could I say? Just imagine how scary it would be for a nine-year-old Vietnamese kid to fly all the way to Wyoming by himself. Especially since he'd have to change planes to get to Jackson Hole."

"You did the right thing, Mom," Ashley told her. "Foster kids are fine. Jack and I will take care of him so you can still have a break. Won't we, Jack?"

Jack nodded, grudgingly. Sheltering foster kids was more his mom's and dad's and sister's idea. Jack preferred to be alone with his family, especially on this fantastic vacation. Still, he nodded and said, "Sure." Speaking cautiously, so his voice wouldn't give too much away, he added, "So when do we have to get this kid?"

"Tomorrow. We'll pick him up on our way to the park."

2

Bright colors were everywhere in Hawaii. It seemed to Jack, looking out from the backseat of the car, as if the sliver of distant ocean melted right into a brass-colored sky. Far below them was a sandy beach that was neither white nor tan, but black. Pure black sand, created, their father told them, when hot lava hit cold ocean waves and exploded into tiny bits of sand.

Alongside the highway, greenery sprang up as thick and lush as velvet. Every few miles Jack would catch a glimpse of a scarlet bird that fluttered and dipped its head into heavy blossoms, just the way hummingbirds hovered around feeders back home.

Once he'd asked his dad to stop the rental car along the side of the road so they could both take pictures of the red bird, but his father said they didn't have time for that just then. They were on their way to pick up Danny.

Turning to face Jack and Ashley in the backseat, their mother told them, "According to these directions, we're almost at the Trans' farm. Now remember, this little boy might be very shy—be prepared for his not talking much. I don't even know how much English he speaks." As he half-listened, Jack was struck by the many strands of dark hair that coiled like sweater fuzz from the top of his mother's normally smooth head. Hawaiian humidity was bringing out the waves in both Olivia's and Ashley's hair, although Jack's blond hair, like his father's, stayed perfectly straight.

"Are you with me, Jack?"

"Me? Yeah." Jack tried to pull his mind back to his mother's voice.

"Jack's not, but I am, Mom," Ashley broke in, pleased with herself. "You said Danny might not speak much English and that he will sleep on an extra cot in our condo living room. You said you don't think he'll be any trouble at all."

"Right. But remember, Danny may be very emotional about leaving Hawaii. I understand he's lived here since he was six. So what I'm trying to say is be extra nice. See if you can draw him out."

"Put yourself in his place," Steven added. "Try to get him to talk about himself, without prying."

"We'll try hard, Dad," Ashley promised.

"Yeah, and if he doesn't talk much, that'll give Ashley a chance to yak even more than she usually does. Danny won't know what hit him," Jack added.

Ashley dug her elbow into Jack's ribs. "Excuse me? I don't either talk all the time," she told him, narrowing her eyes.

"Yeah," Jack snorted. "Right."

"I don't!"

Grinning, Jack turned away from his sister to look out the window. Sometimes he liked to annoy her just to watch her defend herself. It wasn't that her jabbering really bothered him; Jack was a little envious of the ease Ashley had with people. There was something in her cheerful manner, in how she could take a quiet person's hand and coax him out of himself, that Jack couldn't quite understand. But the truth was, he would rather take pictures of people than find out about their insides. In the end, it all came down to the fact that he was happy to let the foster kids fall under Ashley's care.

Leaning as far forward as she could with her seat belt on, Ashley tapped Olivia's shoulder. "Mom, Jack says I'm a chatterbox, but I don't think that's right. Do you think I am?"

Olivia hesitated. "I think you're an excellent communicator. If Danny is shy, you're the one who will make him feel comfortable."

Ashley wasn't satisfied. "I know I'm supposed to be good with people and all that. But that's not what I'm asking. Do you think I talk too much? Because if I do, I think I should know how you really feel. Dad—"

"I think we make a right turn here," Steven interrupted loudly, trying to change the subject. "There's the name on the mailbox. See, Ashley? Tran Dinh Hien."

"Wait a second. I thought Danny's last name was Tran." Ashley looked puzzled.

"It is," Jack told her. "Vietnamese people put their last names first. There was a Vietnamese kid in my class when I was in fourth grade. My teacher explained how they do it."

"But Mom said this boy's name is Danny Tran. So his last name comes last, not first."

"They probably Americanized it," Steven answered, turning into a dirt driveway. "This place isn't very big, is it?"

They were used to widespread Wyoming ranches that covered hundreds of acres. The Tran farm was small enough to be fenced all the way around. Chickens scratched the surface of a flat, neat yard with an ornate birdbath in the middle. A house no bigger than the Landons' garage in Jackson Hole sat at the end of the dirt driveway, shaded from the hot sun by tall eucalyptus trees.

Since a light rain had just finished falling,

the trees' leaves still dripped moisture.

"Look at those gorgeous flowers," Olivia exclaimed. "Oh, I love birds of paradise." She pointed to the vividly colored blooms lining the drive. "Birds of paradise and—I don't even know what the rest of these flowers are called, but— over there! Those are orchids, aren't they? Imagine growing orchids in your own yard. Beautiful!"

The door of the neat house banged open and a small, wiry boy with thick black hair ran toward them. A pair of blue shorts skimmed his knees, while his perfectly matching red, white, and blue striped shirt and white sneakers made him look, to Jack, like an American flag. Every hair was combed neatly in place, and his skin gleamed from a fresh scrubbing.

"Hi! Are you the Landons?" he shouted, even before they could get the car doors open. "I'm Danny. I'm going to fly back to the mainland with you. Come on, get out. Aunt Lan has lunch waiting, and Uncle Hien wants to talk to you. He can't speak English. I have to translate, so make sure you talk where I can hear, and I'll tell them what you say. How do you like it in Hawaii? Is Wyoming like here?" Danny had stopped directly in front of Jack. "How old are you?"

So much for "shy," Jack thought. The kid hadn't even stopped for a breath. "I'm twelve."

"Twelve? Cool! You're really tall for twelve."

"Yeah, I guess, sort of," Jack answered.

"No, really. I thought you were at least fifteen."

Jack smiled broadly. He liked it when people thought he was older than he was.

But fifteen?

"Do you play basketball? I bet you do, if your school's got a team. Does it? I bet you're on the A-team, right? What's your name?"

Since he couldn't remember all the questions Danny had peppered him with, Jack answered the last one.

"I'm Jack," he said slowly, "and this is—"

But before he could introduce the rest of the family, Danny talked on.

"I know your last name's Landon, but the woman from Social Services didn't tell me your first name. I'm nine, but I'm in fifth grade because I got skipped a year."

"Wow," Jack answered, mainly because he didn't know what else to say.

"So, do you like Nintendo? I really love it, even though my aunt and uncle don't like me to play. What's your favorite—?"

Steven held out his hand, palm up, as if to stop Danny's flood of words, then reached out for a handshake. "I'm Steven, the father," he said. "This is my wife, Olivia, you've met our son, Jack, and this is our daughter, Ashley. We're glad to meet you, Danny."

Ashley beamed at Danny, but he didn't seem to notice. His dark eyes were trained exclusively on Jack.

"Do you eat spring rolls? I told Aunt Lan she should fix them because Americans are funny about eating things like eel soup."

"Eel soup? The kind of eels that swim in the ocean and look like snakes?" Ashley began, wiggling her hand sideways as if it were a serpent. "Yuck. I didn't know anyone really made soup out of those things—"

But Ashley had to swallow the rest of her sentence because Danny talked right over the top of her words. "Have you ever tried it?"

"No," Ashley answered meekly.

"Then why do you say 'yuck?' There's not anything different between eating an eel and eating a tuna fish. They both swim in the ocean and stuff. I bet Jack would eat eel if we had some. Right, Jack?"

"Maybe. But spring rolls sound great," he answered, relieved that his manners wouldn't be put to that kind of test.

"Oh come on, Jack," Ashley said, incredulous. "You wouldn't eat an eel and you know it. You won't even eat broccoli."

"That's because I already know what broccoli tastes like."

"So you're saying you'd actually chew on a

piece of eel?" Ashley's eyebrows were halfway up her forehead.

"I might."

"Ashley, Jack," Olivia interrupted, giving them a warning look. "Why don't we go inside now? I'd like to meet the rest of Danny's family."

"You know what? I hate broccoli too," Danny said, beaming at Jack. "I think we're a lot alike."

Just then the door opened, and two small, ancient-looking people came out onto the narrow porch. They smiled and bowed.

Danny said something in Vietnamese to them. To the Landons, he announced, "This is my uncle Hien and my aunt Lan. They're saying that your family honors our house by your visit. Come on and talk to them, Jack. I bet they'll really like you."

Danny grabbed Jack's hand and pulled him toward the house. The rest of them fell in line, with a frowning Ashley trailing at the back.

The door frame was low enough that Steven, who stood six feet three, had to duck his head to go inside.

In the small, formal living room, the same tropical flowers that bloomed along the driveway filled vases resting on almost every surface.

"Sit, please," Danny instructed, while the tiny, wrinkled woman spread her hands and nodded, urging them toward the chairs.

Both she and her husband wore dark cotton

tunics. Aunt Lan's, however, was embroidered with birds the color of flame.

"She's your aunt?" Ashley asked.

"Wrong. You got it all wrong," Danny said in a singsongy voice. "Guess again."

Jack saw Ashley's lips press together briefly before she answered, "OK, I got it. She's your great-aunt."

"Wrong again! She's my *great-great* aunt. And he's my great-great uncle. That's why they're sending me to the U. S. mainland. They say they're too old now to raise a boy." Turning to Jack, he added, "Ever since Aunt Lan fell down and hurt her hip, it's been extra hard for her to walk. See how she limps on her right leg? I try to help her as much as I can, but she's eighty-three years old and Uncle Hien is eighty-seven. They say I need more than they can give. So they decided to send me to my grandpa in Wyoming. I don't know him."

Jack thought Danny would be a handful for even much younger people. There went his mother's peaceful vacation. And his. They were going to have to spend three more days with this talkative, wired-up kid before the family flew back to Wyoming. Still, Jack couldn't help noticing the way Danny looked at him. It was as if Jack were a lot more important than his parents or Ashley. Maybe that part wasn't so bad.

Aunt Lan brought out bowls of noodles and

plates of spring rolls, insisting with gestures that her guests eat heartily. After she offered them chopsticks, and all four Landons struggled to hold them properly, the old woman's face wreathed in wrinkles of amusement. A moment later, Aunt Lan returned bearing forks and spoons.

To make polite conversation, Steven turned to the old man and asked, "What sorts of crops do you raise here on the farm?"

After Danny interpreted, Uncle Hien gave a very long, involved answer, which Danny then translated as, "ginger root."

Steven had to laugh. "Aw, come on now, Danny," he protested. "He must have said more than that."

"Yeah, what'd he say?" Ashley added.

"Do you really want to know all of it?" Although the question belonged to Steven, or maybe Ashley, Danny's eyes darted toward Jack. Steven gave a slight nod, so Jack shrugged and said, "Sure."

"Well, Uncle Hien said ginger is excellent for the digestion and for many other things, like seasickness, women's cramps, and headaches. And that because of ginger he—Uncle Hien—has lived a long and healthy life and hopes he will live many years longer. But Aunt Lan is having trouble with her bones, and all the ginger he gives her doesn't seem able to cure that."

All four Landons remained speechless, not sure

what to answer. Then the old woman murmured something.

"My aunt Lan says, you little children—she means you, Jack and Ashley—must surely like ginger ale, because all children like ginger ale. And didn't you ever wonder how ginger ale is made? It's from ginger root."

The old woman shuffled off again, swaying awkwardly to one side. Soon she returned, both hands full of what looked like a bunch of carrots all stuck together, but lumpier, and tan instead of orange. She presented them like an offering to Olivia.

"Thank you," Olivia said, smiling and giving a little bow. "Please tell her, Danny, that as soon as we get home to Jackson Hole, I'll look up some recipes for ginger."

While Danny translated, and Aunt Lan smiled and nodded, a sleek, silver-gray cat padded into the room and wound around the old woman's legs. Reaching down slowly, she patted the top of the cat's head with trembling fingers.

"That's Minh Nu, our cat. Do you like cats, Jack?" Danny asked.

"Yeah. Sure." Suddenly Jack thought of a joke he'd heard. "What do you get when you plant a cat?"

"I don't know. What?"

"A fur tree. Get it? F-u-r tree."

Danny's laughter rang out loud and long, as though that was the most hilarious thing that had ever been said. "Fur tree! You're really funny."

Both his great-great-aunt and his great-great-uncle frowned severely until Danny covered his mouth with his hand, stifling his giggles. Clearing his throat, he said, "They beg you not to blame them for my terrible manners. They say it's the American schools that have ruined all my natural Vietnamese courtesy."

Ashley wrinkled her forehead. "American? I thought you went to school here in Hawaii."

"Hawaii *is* part of the United States of America," Danny told her. "It's the fiftieth state, added August twenty-first, nineteen fifty-nine. Don't you know about your own country, Ashley? There are eight islands in the Hawaiian chain—and this one's the biggest. I bet Jack knew that."

Ashley dug her fingernails into Jack's bare arm. "Ouch!" Jack said. What was bugging Ashley?

As the bright blue car wound around curves on the way to the park, Ashley, Jack, and Danny kept bumping into one another in the narrow backseat. Since getting into the car, Danny had been quiet, which threw Jack off almost more than his chatter.

The parting on the small front porch, when Danny said good-bye to his great-great-aunt and great-great-uncle, had been tearful. The old man gave Danny money, and the old woman pressed a medal into his hands. Once they were in the car, Danny told the Landons that the medal had belonged to his American grandfather. Then he turned his face to the window and said nothing more.

For once, Ashley hadn't seemed interested in filling the space left by the silence. To break it, Jack asked, "How long will we stay in the park, Mom?"

"About four or five hours. I'll be meeting with the park's wildlife biologist and some scientists from the university."

"Why'd you come all the way to Hawaii for a meeting that lasts only four or five hours?"

"We're going to exchange ideas and data and make some plans for a future conference. Lots of times," Olivia explained, "information becomes much clearer when you talk to people face to face. Darcy—she's the biologist—has charts and films and live specimens to show all of us. They would have been impossible for her to mail out."

"Live specimens of what, Mom?" Ashley wanted to know. Those were the first words she'd spoken since she'd left the Tran house. Maybe all that teasing about her being a chatterbox upset her more than Jack had guessed.

"Nēnē."

"Neigh neigh sounds like what a horse would say."

"Very funny, Ashley," Olivia answered. "Nēnē are geese."

"I know all about nēnē," Danny announced, emerging from his island of silence. "This is the only place in the world where they're found. They were almost extinct, then some people got the last thirty nēnē that were left and started breeding them. Now there's a couple hundred of them here on this island."

Jack was impressed. Danny seemed to be one smart kid.

"So what do nēnē geese look like?" Ashley asked.

"Don't say 'nēnē geese,'" Danny corrected her. "In the Hawaiian language, 'nēnē' means 'geese,' so if you say 'nēnē geese' it's like saying 'geese geese.' Also, you don't say 'nēnēs' when you mean more than one. Just 'nēnē.' It's like you don't say 'fishes' when you mean more than one fish. You say 'two fish' or 'three fish,' and it's the same thing, like 'two nēnē' or 'three nēnē.'"

Ashley moved over.

Farther away from Danny.

"How much longer till we get there, Dad?" she asked.

"Not long, judging from the map. We'll drop off your mother at the park wildlife building,"

Steven told her, "and then you kids and I will drive around to explore a little."

"If you want to know about Hawaii Volcanoes National Park," Danny said, sounding like his old self again, "just ask me. I came here a lot. I can show you all the best places."

"I want to see a volcano erupt," Ashley told him.

"Maybe you can," Danny said. "The only way to see that for sure is if Pele lets you."

"Who's Pele?" Jack asked.

"I know," Ashley began. "She's—"

Before she could say another word, Danny broke in, "She's the goddess of all the volcanoes in Hawaii. She decides when a volcano's going to erupt. There's no big eruption going on right now, but if you want to see a gigantic crater, we can go to Kilauea Iki overlook. Once when Kilauea Iki erupted, the lava shot nineteen hundred feet into the air."

Exasperated, Ashley asked, "How do you know so much about everything?"

"I have a super photographic memory," Danny explained. "If I read something once, I remember it forever. That's why I'm so smart."

Jack noticed Ashley's hands. They were clenched into tight fists. Still, she kept her voice pleasant as she said, "That's really great, Danny."

"Yeah, I wish I could do that," Jack added. "I

bet you ace all your tests in school."

"I do," Danny agreed. "Lots of times I know more than the teacher. I bet you're like that, too, Jack. You're really smart, I can tell."

Ashley rolled her eyes toward the ceiling of the car.

Jack swallowed a grin. He was really beginning to like Danny.

They pulled up beside a kiosk, where a park ranger asked to see their visitor's pass. Instead, Olivia showed him her letter from Darcy, the biologist, and the ranger waved them on.

"We'll stop at park headquarters first," she told them. "I'll call Darcy from there and get directions on how to reach the wildlife building."

Ashley sat coiled as if she wanted to explode from the car, but since it was a two-door, she, Jack, and Danny had to wait for the adults to get out of the front seat first.

Once all of them were standing on the asphalt of the parking lot, Ashley maneuvered Jack out of hearing range of the others.

"I can't take much more of that Danny," she hissed. "He's such a know-it-all. I mean, he's in fifth grade like me, but he's a whole year younger than I am. He thinks he's some kind of brainiac." Stepping back, she jerked her fingers through her dark, curly hair. "Plus, he either ignores me or talks right over what I'm saying or else tells me I'm wrong about stuff. Ugh! And what is the deal with the way he's acting toward you? It's like you're some kind of hero or something."

"Nah. It's just a guy thing," Jack said lamely. "Besides, I think he really is smart."

"And that mouth! I mean, you said I talked too much, and he's ten times worse than I ever was. Don't you think he's obnoxious?"

"He's kind of a pain, I guess."

Ashley nodded vigorously.

"But he's not too bad," Jack carefully added. Danny, three years younger, was a good 12 inches shorter and 40 pounds lighter than Jack. So what if he was brainy? He wasn't any kind of a threat to Jack, a seventh grader. In fact, Danny amused him. And he had to admit that he kind of warmed to the way the kid admired him. It was like rescuing a lost puppy that followed you around begging for attention. "Maybe you need to lighten up a little, Ashley," Jack said.

"J-a-a-c-k," Danny cried out. "What are you doing with Ashley? I want you to see the red bird. It's called a Hawaiian honeycreeper. Hurry up."

"You go on," Ashley said, waving her hand to dismiss Jack. "Mom and Dad and I will be right behind you."

They all trooped into park headquarters.

While Olivia was on the phone, Steven studied some detailed maps of the park.

"You don't need a map," Danny said. "I know my way around. Just tell me where you want to go, and I'll show you how to drive there."

Steven smiled at him. "Just to be sure, I'd better get a map. You may not need one, Danny, but I will if we all get lost from one another."

Steven was only joking. But later, Jack would wish his father had never spoken those words.

3

I know exactly where we should go," Danny announced. "It's called Devastation Trail. It looks like the land of the living dead!" Danny's dark eyes sparkled as he added, "It's the spookiest place in Hawaii!"

"Spooky, huh? It does sound interesting, Danny," Steven told him as the car rolled along through yet another lush stretch of green. Olivia had already headed off with Darcy, the biologist, leaving the four of them to discover more of the park on their own. "But if it's all right with you, I kind of want to photograph Puu Puai. I hear it's got a pretty interesting cinder cone, and maybe some of those nēnē Mom's been talking about." Looking at Danny in the rearview mirror, he added, "I'd love to get a really good shot of a nēnē."

Steven Landon was an almost professional

photographer. He couldn't earn a living just by taking pictures, so he worked in a photo shop. Every extra cent he could afford, he spent on good camera equipment, and every opportunity that came his way, he photographed wildlife.

"Then you should park at Puu Puai overlook. The nēnē are there," Danny responded. "Jack—did you know that the nēnē is the Hawaiian state bird?"

"I knew that," murmured Ashley, who sat in the front seat of the car. "I learned it at the visitors' center." From the stiff way she held her head, Jack could tell she was still ticked. Every word out of Danny's mouth seemed to irritate her like biting flies.

Steven, sensing Ashley's mood, reached over to pat her head and spoke to her in soft words Jack couldn't quite make out.

Danny leaned forward, thrusting his face between Ashley's and Steven's. "You know what, Mr. Landon? You can drop us kids off at the Devastation Trail parking lot and then drive over to Puu Puai by yourself so you can get your pictures. Devastation Trail starts at the parking lot and ends at the Puu Puai overlook. From the overlook you can get a good view of the cinder cone and a really great view of Kilauea Iki Crater. You'll like Kilauea Iki, I guarantee it. And us kids can hike across the trail and meet you at Puu Puai."

Ashley said, "Icky-poo-poo. Dad, how come all the names around here sound so funny?" She wrinkled her nose.

"They just sound different to you 'cause you're a haole," Danny told her, with a small, superior smile.

Ashley frowned at him. "A haole? What's that?"

"It's a Hawaiian word that means you're white and from the mainland. See, Hawaiian names sound strange to most haole, because the Hawaiian language has only twelve letters in the whole alphabet, and all their words have to end in a vowel and—"

"You can stop now, Danny," Ashley said a little too loudly. "You don't have to give a lecture about everything. Sometimes people are just talking, you know? And I was talking to my dad, not to you."

"Ashley," Steven said quietly. "Come on, now."

"Oh," Danny said, a bit subdued. "I thought you wanted to know about the names, but I guess I do talk too much. My aunt and uncle tell me I talk too much. They say my mouth runs like the Mekong River in flood." Danny gave a weak laugh, which withered and died on the floor of the car.

Jack was staying out of it, at least for now. He

kept his head turned, looking out the window. Sun floated underneath clouds the color of pewter, casting shadows across the road like a dark curtain.

To Jack, the tension that hung between Danny and Ashley felt like that heavy curtain, cutting each of them off from the other, and it made Jack uncomfortable. He didn't have the slightest idea how to improve things between them, since the interworkings of people had always been Ashley's territory, not his. He was relieved when he saw the sign pointing to the Devastation Trail parking area.

"Well, this must be the place," Steven announced brightly. He slid the car to an easy stop between two yellow lines in the empty parking area. "So..." Steven hesitated. "It's OK with you, Ashley, isn't it, if we do what Danny suggested?"

"I don't care," she said, giving a tiny shrug.

"All right, then." Unfolding the map he'd picked up at park headquarters, Steven leaned it against the steering wheel and let his finger trace a thin, broken line that crossed the paper like a tiny vein.

"It shows here that the trail is only half a mile long, so by the time you kids hike from here to Puu Puai overlook, I should have enough pictures of the crater, and of any nēnē I can find." Looking at his watch, he said, "It's almost two-thirty now.

Jack—is your watch set on Hawaii time?"

"Yep, four hours behind Jackson Hole time."

"Great. What say we meet in half an hour?"

"Sure, Dad," Jack said. "Come on, Ashley."

"No." Steven held up his hand. "You boys go on outside and wait for just a minute. I want to talk to Ashley alone."

"Am I in trouble?" she asked, her eyes wide.

Steven ran his fingers through his thinning blond hair. "Nah, I just want to talk, that's all. OK, guys, hop on out. Ashley and I will only be a second."

From where the boys stood, a dozen yards from the car, it was like seeing a movie with the sound turned off. To keep the conversation private, the car's windows had been rolled up. Ashley's hands flew wildly through the air as she talked, while Steven's hands moved deliberately, calmly.

Danny watched, frowning, his lips pressed together. Finally he said, "Ashley doesn't like me."

"Sure she does," Jack lied.

"It's OK. Some kids don't like me all that much. I'm used to it." Danny's voice sounded flat, almost matter of fact. It seemed as if he were speaking of someone else rather than himself. "When I was in camp, I had just one friend, Duong Le. He was your age. He—he was a lot like you, Jack." He stared off into the distance, his eyes clouding with memory. "Since Duong Le, I haven't had a really good friend."

Jack wrinkled his brow. "Camp? What camp?"

Danny shivered as if a cool breeze were passing over his skin. "Forget I said anything. Look," he said, pointing to the car. "I think they're done. Now we can hike."

Jack saw that inside the car, Steven was reaching over to give Ashley a hug. Ashley looked in Jack's direction, nodded a few times, then got out of the car and waved as Steven pulled away.

Neither Jack nor his sister had on hiking boots, just regular sneakers, but that should be OK, Jack thought, because they were going to walk for less than a mile. Both of them wore camping shorts—broken-in denim that had become soft and faded from repeated washings—and cotton T-shirts: Jack's had rainbow-colored fish swimming across the front, while Ashley's shirt was splashed with bright birds.

The thin cotton wouldn't provide much protection from sunburn, but then, the sun had barely broken through the clouds for the past hour.

Ashley's hair blew off her face as she walked toward them. Her eyes were focused resolutely on the ground.

"Wait here, Danny," Jack told him. "I want to talk to Ashley."

"It's about me, isn't it?" Danny began.

"Just wait."

When Danny was far enough behind him, Jack whispered into Ashley's ear, "What did Dad say?"

"He said I needed to give Danny a break, because he's had a lot of bad stuff in his life. I asked him what it was, but he wouldn't tell me. But I don't know what could have been so bad. I mean, his aunt and uncle seemed really nice."

"Come on, Jack," Danny called through cupped hands. "This is the hiking trail I was telling you about. After a while, it gets really, really creepy!"

As they walked slowly along the trail, their footsteps crunched as if they were tramping on a concrete floor coated with potato chips.

"Hey, Danny, how come this gravelly stuff's all over the place?" Jack asked.

"It's from Pele," Danny answered.

"Pele?"

"The goddess of the volcano. Remember when I told you how Kilauea Iki erupted that time? It threw up cinders sky-high, and then the cinders fell down like rain for miles around. That's what we're walking on—the layer of cinders. And Pele was the one who put them here."

Jack picked up a handful. They weren't all black; some of them were rust colored. "They're light," he said. "In weight, I mean."

"Yep. Sometimes they'll even float, if you put them on water. But wait'll you see what's up ahead. Bones from dead animals. Thousands and thousands of them. Scary!"

They crunched farther down the path. In front of them, bleached branches of bare, dead trees clutched at the sky like gnarled fingers. The dark ground was littered with white lengths of—bone? According to Danny, that's what it was. The pieces ranged in length from hand size to twisted stakes six feet long. It looked as though a whole herd of prehistoric creatures had died there and left their skeletons behind: leg bones, ribs, vertebrae, all vivid against the dark cinders.

"See? Aren't they spooky?" Danny asked.

Ashley breathed softly. "They're real bones, aren't they?"

Danny laughed, loud and long, and this time he didn't bother to cover his mouth with his hand. "Real bones? No way. They're pieces of dead trees—and you couldn't tell the difference! I fooled you! Duh!"

"Listen, you little—"

"Ssshhhhh!" Danny hissed. "Over there. Nēnē." He pointed to a low bush about 20 feet ahead of them. A bill, two eyes, and a neck that looked like a thick, spiral-twisted rope poked out first, followed by the rest of the plump tan and brown bird. As it marched forward from behind the bush, Jack realized where the term "goose step" came from.

Head down, the nēnē nibbled the top of a stalk of grass. Then, with its shiny black bill, it clipped off a whole grass blade at the base and ate it like a kid sucking up a strand of spaghetti.

"Maybe it has babies hidden in there," Jack whispered.

Another nēnē stepped out of the bush, lifting one webbed foot and then the other, setting them down precisely in line. Jack said softly, "Both its legs are banded. One white band, one red. I guess Mom's friend Darcy has already captured that nēnē and put the bands on its legs to identify it."

"Can we get closer?" Ashley whispered. The sight of the strange birds made her forget some of her anger at Danny.

"Don't know. Try to. Walk slow and soft."

Walking softly was impossible on the crunchy cinders, but both of them moved as carefully as they could. The two nēnē didn't seem especially concerned, yet for every step forward Jack and Ashley took, the geese managed to move away from them by about the same distance. They seemed to take turns feeding, one casually nibbling at plants while the other nēnē watched, bright black eyes peering out of a black face, always keeping the human visitors in view.

Jack realized the birds' necks looked twisted because the feathers were furrowed, as though someone had run fingers through the neck feathers while they were wet.

Danny hung back, out of eye range, seeming uninterested. Jack guessed he'd seen lots of nēnē in the three years he'd lived in Hawaii.

But Jack was plenty interested. His small point-and-shoot camera hung from a strap around his neck. He pushed the button that slid back the lens cover, wishing it didn't make that little squealing sound when it opened, but the geese paid no attention. Even though the day was overcast, there was enough light that he wouldn't need to use the built-in flash, which was good, because a flash going off might startle the nēnē.

"You finished?" Danny asked loudly after Jack had taken half a dozen pictures. "Wow! I figured your dad was a photographer, but I didn't know you were, too."

"Not really," Jack said. "Maybe someday."

"Come on over here. I want you to try something." Danny pointed to a different kind of bush than the one the nēnē had hidden in. "See these berries? Go ahead, eat them."

"You're not allowed to pick things in a national park," Jack declared. Almost from babyhood, Jack and Ashley had had drummed into their ears the motto "In our national parks, take nothing but photographs; leave behind nothing except your footprints." He would never dare to pick a flower or a leaf or even swipe a small, insignificant stone, because in a national park, everything really was significant.

"Wrong," Danny told them. "In this park you're allowed to pick 'ōhelo berries."

"I don't believe you," Ashley said hotly. "It's—it's—a *sin* to hurt nature in a place like this. Dad says we're in charge of you, and I say you can't pick them."

"I can't?" Danny's dark eyes flashed. "Just watch me."

The leaves of the 'ōhelo bush were dark green and round. The 'ōhelo berries looked like tiny, shiny red apples, but waxy, and squashable.

Danny picked a dozen berries, one after the other, and shoved all of them into his mouth at the same time.

Ashley's eyes narrowed, her nostrils flared, and she glowered.

"Mmmmm, tastes like Sweetarts," Danny said. "I swear to you, it's OK to eat them. Come on, Jack. Try one."

Jack hesitated.

"I better not," he said. "Just in case."

"But it's all right. Honest! Know why? Because 'ōhelo berries are sacred to Pele, and if the native Hawaiians weren't allowed to pick them here, there'd be a lot of trouble. It's like—religion. So that means everyone else gets to pick them, too."

"Who's this Pele you keep talking about?" Jack asked, trying to get Danny's mind off of eating the 'ōhelo berries.

The three of them hadn't been hiking more than ten minutes, and already Ashley's irritation was building like lava, getting ready to erupt. How was he going to keep these two from killing each other on the rest of the hike? Suddenly, 20 more minutes seemed like a long, long time.

"Let me tell you all about Pele, Jack," Danny said, ignoring Ashley. "Pele was—"

"Hold on! I know this story!" Ashley declared. "When I found out we were coming on this trip, I checked out a whole lot of books about Hawaii. I read about Pele. Sit down here next to the 'ōhelo bush and I'll tell the legend. And Danny, don't you dare interrupt me!"

4

Pele was the queen of the sacred fire. Her older sister controlled the seas.

When Pele made the long voyage from Tahiti, where she was born, her jealous sister chased her all the way across the blue waters. But Pele stayed safe, because a great shark protected her canoe.

After many months on the ocean, Pele at last reached the northernmost island of the Hawaiian chain. There she found a crater where she could hide her sacred fires of creation. All too soon, though, her sister came and drenched the fires with seawater, drowning the flames.

But Pele managed to save just enough of the sacred fire to start over again. Carrying the embers with her, she moved first from one island and then to another, making her way south along all the islands in the Hawaiian chain.

At each place, she would dig a crater to make a home for herself, where she could guard the fire. Then her elder sister would come and destroy it. Again and again, on one island after another, the sister poured pounding seas over Pele's flames, turning them into clouds of steam that blew away in the wind.

At last Pele's wrath grew as hot as her fire.

On Maui, the next to last island, her fury drove her into a battle with her sister. The fight between the two woman was so violent it exploded into raging lava and roaring waves. Steam hissed, thunder burst, lightning stabbed the ground and earthquakes shook it. Yet neither of the two women seemed able to defeat the other.

The older sister, desperate, called on a sea monster to come and help her. That was too much! Pele couldn't save herself. The sea monster tore her into pieces. Her bones are still on Maui.

Yet death had freed Pele's spirit. Soon after, the Hawaiian people noticed a rosy glow above the Mauna Loa volcano on the southernmost, and biggest, island of Hawaii. The whole sky blazed, brighter than the most brilliant sunrise or sunset, with every shade of fiery color human eyes had ever seen. It was Pele's spirit, soaring overhead like a flaming rainbow. That was how the people knew that Pele had become a goddess. The goddess of volcanoes. The goddess of fire.

She was beautiful, with long hair that flowed like black ropes of lava, and eyes that burned like coals. But sometimes Pele would disguise herself as a bent old woman.

One time, a handsome young warrior named Paoa stood on the edge of a crater and looked down. Far below him, on the crater floor, he saw four beautiful women seated on slabs of pāhoehoe lava.

From where Paoa stood, he was unable to see that there was a fifth woman, old and withered and bent, who had hidden herself in a cave at the bottom of the crater.

"Come down, come down," the beautiful women called to him. Their voices were like music to Paoa. He climbed down the walls of the crater until he reached them.

"Where is Pele?" he asked them.

The four women began to tease him. "This one is Pele," they said, pointing to one another. "Or maybe this one. Or maybe I am Pele." And they laughed at him.

"I know how I can tell which one is Pele," Paoa said.

He took the hand of the first woman and held it to his cheek. "No, not you," he told her, and picked up the hand of the second woman. "Not you, either."

After he'd raised the hands of each of the four

women to his cheek, Paoa turned to the old hag, who'd come creeping out of the crater's cave. "Give me your hand," he demanded.

She pulled back. "If none of these beautiful young women is Pele, how can you think that a wrinkled old crone like me could be the goddess of the volcano?"

But Paoa took her hand anyway—and immediately dropped it, because it was burning hot.

"You are Pele!" he cried in triumph. At that, Pele turned back into her beautiful self, and they all celebrated with a feast of roast pig, poi, and papaya. The end.

"Did you like that? Isn't that a great story?" Ashley asked. "I made up the 'pig, poi, and papaya' part because I don't know what they really ate, but Mom told me those foods are Hawaiian."

"The story's nice, yeah," Danny said, "because you left out all the scary stuff about how Pele killed everybody. You forgot all the best parts! Anyone messed with Pele, and pow! She'd zap 'em into cinders. That's why Paoa came to Kilauea, because he was looking for the body of his best friend that Pele killed, and you know why she killed the guy? Because he paid attention to another woman. That was enough to make Pele turn him into red-hot barbecue."

"Danny, do you have to mess up everything?"

Ashley cried. "I was telling the story. It was a nice story until you ruined it."

"I'm just saying what's true. Any time Pele got mad at anyone, she'd pour hot lava over them. Charcoal grilled. With fries." He laughed at his own joke. "And Pele didn't just go after people. She burned trees and houses and pigs and dogs and—"

"Stop it!" Ashley stomped her foot like a kindergarten teacher trying to control rowdy five-year-olds. "You're making me crazy!"

Looking totally innocent, Danny asked, "What'd I do?"

He's not faking, Jack thought. He really doesn't know how much he's bothering her.

Jack couldn't figure out how to make things right between them, didn't know a way to sort out the tangle of feelings that had sprung up like poison ivy. It was clear Danny and Ashley didn't get along, the same way Pele and her sister tried to burn and drown each other. The sooner Jack could get them apart, the better.

"That was a good story, Ashley," he said, slapping his hands on the bare skin of his knees. "But I think we'd better shove off now. Dad'll get worried if we're too late, plus it looks like rain. So, uh, no more storms between you guys," he added lamely.

"Wait a minute. What about my part of the

legend? Didn't you like the stuff I said about how Pele fried people?" Danny looked at Jack and smiled. His teeth were square and white.

"Yeah," Jack quickly agreed. "That was cool, too."

Folding her arms across her chest, Ashley focused her words on Jack alone. "Except don't you think the story was better without the killing part? I mean, to me, what Danny said ruined the legend. It was really nice until he started adding all that stuff about burning people alive. Don't you think I'm right, Jack?"

Warmth began to rise through Jack's skin.

Cornered. That's how he felt. Danny on one side, pulling at him, his sister on the other, silently begging Jack to stand with her.

Thunder rumbled overhead, maybe giving him an easy out. Holding his hand palm up, Jack squinted at the sky. "Is that a drop I felt? We'd better go."

"Right. But, I still want to know what you think." Ashley shot a look at Danny, then slid her eyes back onto Jack's. "Which way was it better?"

Jack shrugged. "I don't know."

"Mine, 'cause it's true," Danny argued. "You can't just take the bad stuff out of a story to make you feel good."

Ashley's voice was sharp. "What's wrong with that?"

"Because if it's changed, it's not the true legend. It's like real life—bad stuff happens all the time. You take it out, and *that's* when it turns into make-believe."

"What if I don't agree with you?"

"Then you're wrong," Danny said simply.

Jack looked at Ashley, trying with his will to make her give it up.

"Aunt Lan and Uncle Hien are like you. They want me to just remember pretty things. They say memories should be beautiful, like orchids. But even if I don't say them out loud, the memories— they're still there. If I have to remember things differently, it doesn't change anything. It just makes a prettier, make-believe story."

Ashley stuck out her chin. She didn't answer him. Jack had the strange feeling that there was a conversation within the conversation, something that Danny hid beneath a layer of words, like nesting toys stacked one inside the other. It was in the way Danny stood, his small body stiff, his dark eyes flashing with intensity, that made Jack wonder if Danny was talking about more than Pele.

"I guess you're that way too, aren't you, Jack?" Danny asked softly. "Like Ashley, I mean. Wanting to hear only the good stuff?" He was not pleading, the way Ashley had.

Cautiously, not quite allowing his feelings

to show, Danny looked at Jack through half-lowered eyelids.

Draw him out, their parents had said in the car, before they even met Danny. Try to get him to talk about himself. But this was not the time for it. Wind whipped Ashley's hair in her face, and she angrily pulled the dark strands away as she breathed the thick air and waited for Jack to answer.

"We'll talk later," Jack said. "We need to get back to the car before the storm pours buckets on us." He wanted to walk away from this strange conversation, get his body in motion and forget the now discouraged look on Danny's face.

The sky had darkened ominously. Gray clouds rolled in faster than Jack would have thought possible. A low rumble of thunder came from somewhere; it echoed along the cinder paths.

"OK. We go this way," Danny said, starting down the trail at a brisk trot. Reluctantly, almost dragging her feet, Ashley followed him. Jack brought up the rear, striding after the other two down the crooked cinder path. It was lined with the dead-looking white branches. Someone had set those branches end to end in long parallel rows to mark the trail.

"Slow down, Danny," Jack yelled. "We need to stay together."

The hill had turned steep. Halfway down the incline, Danny finally stopped and spun around to face them. Looking impatient, he crossed his arms and said, "So come on, then," as he waited for them to catch up.

A warm, wet wind began to blow. Right above their heads, it seemed, another, much louder crash of thunder reverberated. Danny's eyes grew wide and his lips parted. He dropped his arms and stared.

"What's wrong? Scared of thunder?" Jack asked.

"No, I'm not scared of anything. I'm tough."

"What, then?"

"Just turn around, slow. Look what's behind you."

Above, on the top rim of the hill they'd just descended, stood a large woman. Her long, thick hair was tossed by the wind, making it stand out almost sideways from her face in a billowing black cloud. She wore a loose tunic so red it seemed on fire, even under the stormy sky.

Although they were quite a distance away from her, Jack could see her expression. She looked angry.

As she raised both arms toward the sky, a flash of lightning illuminated the woman's face, her red tunic, and everything surrounding her in a blaze of light.

"She's Pele!" Ashley breathed.

The woman in red tried to shout something,

but her words were lost in the loudest burst of thunder Jack had ever heard.

For a moment the stranger stood poised on the rim of the crater. Then she started moving toward them.

"She's after us," Danny hollered. "Come on! Come on—she's coming!"

"You wait!" Jack shouted. "We've got to stay together."

"It's Pele—run!" Ashley screamed.

"No—hold on!"

Neither of them paid any attention to him. They just kept running, spewing cinders beneath their sneakers like sparks.

The woman appeared to be filled with rage, waving her arms and shouting words Jack didn't understand: *A ilalo o Halema'uma'u, e....Ku! 'Aihue!*

She was not following the trail, but coming straight down the steep embankment, slipping and sliding on the cinders but never losing her balance.

"This is crazy!" Jack muttered as he hurried down the trail, his Nikes pounding, sliding on the cinders underfoot as, ahead of him, Danny and Ashley spun around a zigzag bend. If he didn't follow them, he told himself, he might lose them. What could that strange woman possibly want with the three of them? Who was she? It couldn't be Pele—he didn't believe in any of that stuff.

"*A ilalo o Halema'uma'u, e....Ku! 'Aihue!,*" she shrieked.

Crazy or not, he could feel the short hairs on the back of his neck stand up. The lightning storm filled the air with electricity. Thunder cracked, drowning the cries of the woman.

As he reached the bend in the path, Jack slowed for a second, trying to hear over the pounding of his own blood. She wasn't calling out now. For an instant, he thought she was gone.

Until he heard footsteps hammering behind him.

And they didn't stop.

5

Jack was bigger than the other two kids and his legs were longer. But they had a good head start, and Jack was slowed down because with every step he took, his camera kept banging against his chest. He couldn't fit it into the pocket of his shorts, which meant he had no choice except to leave the camera dangling by its strap around his neck. Holding it against him with one hand as he ran was awkward; it felt off balance, but that was the only way to keep the camera safe.

A full five minutes passed before he caught up with Danny and Ashley.

"What is the matter with you?" he yelled. "Stop running!"

"No—she's after us," Danny cried, and at the same time Ashley shouted, "It's Pele."

"That's not Pele."

"Sure it is. I can feel her," Danny called out. "She wants to fry us."

Those words, and the sense that something was behind them, pricked Jack's skin. Whirling around, he studied the path that led to the top of the hill. No one was there.

"Hurry, Jack," Ashley pleaded.

"Yeah, hurry," Danny echoed.

Jack couldn't accept that the person they'd seen was anything more than an ordinary woman. Why she'd screamed at them was anyone's guess. All he knew for sure was that an agitated human being, not a goddess, had followed them, and now she seemed to be gone. Pointing at Danny, he declared, "You're losing it! That was *not* Pele."

"Whatever. But I'm not hanging around to find out what the strange lady's problem is," Danny said.

He began to sprint ahead again, the heels of his feet almost touching the bottom of his shorts as he ran along the cindery path. Ashley threw a troubled glance back at Jack, then took off after Danny, matching him step for step.

"Wait, Danny," Jack called to his disappearing form. "You know Hawaiian, right? Do you know what the lady was saying?"

Danny stopped and ran in place for the five seconds it took him to answer.

"I only know a couple of words in Hawaiian

and she was talking fast. I couldn't understand."

"Come on, Jack," Ashley urged him. "She might catch us."

"She's—not—here!" Jack had a hard time talking to them because they wouldn't slow down; he kept yelling at the backs of their heads. He put on speed to catch up but it wasn't until the trail leveled off that he reached them.

All at once, it was as if a curtain had been lowered on a stage. The terrain changed from barren cinders to tall, close-together trees. Soft rain began to fall. Drops ran down the leaves like water from a downspout, dripping on Jack's head.

He tucked his camera through the neck of his shirt, but that wouldn't help much if his shirt got soaked.

"I've got a plan," Danny told them. "Duck in these trees."

"Wait a minute, we can't go in there. First of all, in national parks," Jack began, "you're never supposed to go off the marked trails—"

"Do what you want!" Danny exploded. "Go ahead and follow your dumb park rules. Let Pele fry you into charcoal. I'm not letting anyone catch me." Suddenly, Danny's voice became low. "She's still behind us. I know it."

Ashley looked at Jack. "Danny says he isn't scared of her, but I am."

"Oh, come on!" Jack demanded, exasperated.

"Listen to you guys. You can't believe that's Pele. Pele's only a made-up story."

"That woman looks just like the picture of Pele I saw in the book," Ashley declared stubbornly.

"No way, Ashley!" Jack was about to say more to straighten out his sister, but suddenly Danny sprang away from them and into some trees.

"Danny, don't go in there—"

The green seemed to swallow Danny's small figure as if he were a bird. "Come on! We're going to lose him," Jack said.

The trees got closer together, tall and gloomy. Or maybe it was the weather that seemed gloomy, since thunder still rumbled as the rain fell harder.

Ashley and Jack had to follow Danny by sound more than by sight. No longer did a crunch from cinders underfoot betray his whereabouts, because on the forest floor, leafy growth covered the layer of volcanic ash. Fernlike trees, or maybe they weren't trees at all but just extra-tall ferns, grew near enough to one another that Danny had to push their leaves aside to get through. Luckily, the swish of leaves parting and the crack of undergrowth being stepped on made him easy to follow, even though they couldn't see him.

"Why won't he stop?" Jack muttered.

"Because of Pele. You want to know something, Jack? I have a feeling that Danny understood what she said. I think that's why he's so scared."

"Hey, Danny—wait up—" Jack's words were cut off when he got smacked in the face by a wet branch. Through clenched teeth he muttered, "This is stupid."

The forest had become thick enough now that without a compass, there was no way to tell whether they were heading east, where Puu Puai overlook was supposed to be, or north or south or west. They could have accidentally turned around completely, or maybe they were just walking in circles.

It was now well past three o'clock, when the sun should have been dipping in the sky so that Jack could tell where west was, at least. But even if it had been possible to see through the overhead tree canopy, it wouldn't have helped much, because the sun was hidden by rain clouds.

"I'm all wet," Ashley complained. "My shoes feel squishy. We should have worn our hiking boots."

"Except we didn't expect to go on a hike today."

"Hey, wait a second." Ashley pushed her finger to her lips and said, "Shhhh."

"What? Do you hear something?" Jack strained to filter the noise around him.

Verdant treetops rustled in the wind, making a sound like a distant ocean. The heavy air seemed to wrap itself around all other sounds of life, muffling everything but the breeze into stillness.

"Ashley, what is it?"

"Pele's not following us anymore," she said softly. "I think we lost her."

"I told you that way back there." Jack decided not to argue whether or not it was Pele. Whoever she was, at least for a little while she'd been after the three of them. But why? "I wonder what it was all about. I mean, what do you think that woman wanted?"

"I don't know," Ashley answered. "But now we're safe. Where did Danny get to?"

Cupping his hands to his mouth, Jack called, "Danny, where are you?"

"Over here." Danny's voice drifted through to them through the trees, sounding muffled, and as if it could be coming from any direction at all. "I'm trying to find the trail to the overlook."

"You better find it," Jack yelled back.

"He will," Ashley answered, although she spoke with a certain amount of doubt. "Danny says he knows his way around here."

"Yeah, well, Danny says a lot of things."

Jack and Ashley pushed through more undergrowth. Fat drops rolled onto their heads from tall fronds above. Rivulets of water wound their way down Jack's arms and back, as if they were insects creeping along his skin.

It's just water, he told himself as another cold drop slithered onto his hand. Still, the image of bugs wiggled into his mind: ticks that bored into their victims like tiny drills, bloating on blood until they reached the size of 'ōhelo berries; slimy leeches that attached themselves to any exposed flesh. Did those things even exist in Hawaii? Jack wasn't sure. But when a bush he pushed past flicked droplets onto his legs, he slapped at his skin until it stung.

Looking through a leafy branch, he saw Danny up ahead, his hair plastered against his forehead like black fingers.

"Stay right there!" Jack commanded him. "The woman's not following us any more. We've got to turn around, Danny. I think we need to backtrack and try to find the way we came in."

"No, that'll take too long. I've got a better way. Trust me." He broke into a big smile. "I've got a great sense of direction."

"We're already half an hour late meeting Dad," Jack pointed out. "We need to get back onto Devastation Trail pretty soon or we're in trouble. Danny, stay there!"

It was like telling the ocean to stand still. Danny just kept moving.

"OK!" he yelled suddenly from a short distance in front of them. "I told you we'd find the trail again. There it is. I see it."

"Devastation Trail?" Jack asked.

"Not exactly. But we can slide down here and get on—"

"Not exactly Devastation Trail, he says," Jack muttered. "Wait a minute! Did you just say slide down? Where are we?"

"Come have a look." Danny waved his arms like a traffic cop, urging them forward.

When they reached him, Ashley took one glimpse and squealed, "We're on top of a cliff!"

Danny said, "Nah. This is just Byron Ledge. There's the floor of Kilauea Iki Crater right down below us—"

"*Way* below us!"

"—and over there on the right is Puu Puai cinder cone."

Pointing off into the distance, Ashley said, "You mean that huge thing that looks like an orange mountain?"

"It's not as big as a mountain—more like a hill. It just looks big from here," Danny assured her. "So we slide down over the edge, and then we walk across the floor of the crater and climb up the cinder cone—"

Hearing that, Jack was determined to put himself in charge again. Somewhere along the way he'd lost control of the situation. Not any more. "Climb the cinder cone?" he snapped. "Are you totally out of your mind?"

"Look, Puu Puai overlook is right next to the cinder cone, and that's where your dad is waiting. Me and you, Jack, we can go and get your dad. Ashley can wait right here and then we'll come back and get her. I don't think she should walk that far."

"Ooooh!" Ashley glared at Danny. "What—you think I can't keep up with you? I can bury you any day of the week."

"No you can't. Not me! I'm tough," Danny answered.

A flush of red crept up Ashley's face as she sputtered, "I can go farther and faster than you ever dreamed of. Did you ever hike up the side of a glacier? I did."

"Did you ever hike up the side of a volcano with smoke coming out of it?" Danny asked her. "I did."

"Yeah, well, I hiked all the way down the Grand Canyon."

"Come on, Ashley." Jack raised his eyebrows. They'd hiked part of the way, but mostly they'd ridden down on mules.

"Well, maybe not all the way down," she admitted.

"That's nothing! How 'bout—" Danny's eyes narrowed so far they almost disappeared—"trying to escape with rain pounding you and dogs after you and helicopters searching with spotlights, and—soldiers with guns—" He stopped abruptly. Ashley and Jack both stared at him. Jack was startled by the harsh images. Guns? Soldiers? Could that really have happened?

He was about to ask, but then he thought maybe he shouldn't. Get him to talk, his dad had said. But don't pry.

"I don't believe you," Ashley declared flat out. "You're making that up."

Danny shrugged. "Think what you want. Come on, we're wasting time. If you're such a great athlete, then go down the side of the crater with me."

Jack wanted to grab Danny and punch some reality into his head, but before he could make a move, Danny disappeared! For a second the top of his head was visible, then nothing! They could hear his voice rising up, as if he were inside a well. "Hey, Ashley. This isn't hard. Even you can handle it."

It took only a second for a look of determination to flash from Ashley's eyes. Oh-oh, Jack thought.

"No, Ashley, you're not going to—" he began, but before he could stop her, she'd gone over the side, too, squealing as she vanished from view.

"They're both crazy," Jack muttered, but there was no one left to hear him.

From below the cliff he heard a loud

"Ooooohweee" coming from Danny. Or was it Ashley? "Yeeehaw," came the reply.

Taking a deep breath, Jack moved closer to the edge. "No way," he cried out when he stepped off the edge and saw what was actually beneath him. Arms outspread, he started down, half running, half sliding.

The ledge sloped down at a steep angle— probably 60 degrees, Jack thought, but before that probability even had time to gel inside his brain, he was yelling at the top of his lungs. What with the loose cinders and the rain-slicked dirt, it was like sliding down the Matterhorn on a snowboard. Luckily, enough trees grew on the slope that he could catch himself from time to time, grabbing branches to slow his skid.

He attempted to see if Ashley was making it safely, but he couldn't glance up for more than a second because he had to keep looking down at the ground to prevent a catastrophe. It was all he could manage to hold himself upright. The only thought that spun nonstop in his head was "I'm gonna kill Danny! For sure. He's a dead boy."

He reached the bottom and skidded to a stop on a pile of lava rocks as big as chairs.

"Hi, Jack!" Ashley called. Not only did she seem safe and sound, she was actually grinning. "Wow!" she exclaimed. "What a ride."

"Wasn't that cool, Jack?" Danny asked, spinning

around on top of a sofa-size hunk of lava, with his arms outstretched, bobbing and weaving. "I saw you going like this—boom, ba-boom, bump. Me, I thought it was great. Like a roller coaster without any up parts."

"Did you see me, Jack?" Ashley wanted to know. "Part of the way down I skidded on my bottom, but mostly I could stand up straight. It was fun!"

"*Fun!*"

"Yeah. Maybe it wasn't as much fun for you because you're tall like Dad and your hair kinda got caught in some of the branches, 'cause I saw you grabbing at them. But Danny and I were short enough to duck underneath."

"You're short on brains, too!" Jack yelled at them. "Both of you. That was dangerous. We could have broken bones."

"Oh, lighten up, Jack," Ashley said. "That's what you told me, remember? It was only an hour or so ago when you said it to me, but it seems a lot longer, doesn't it?"

Danny had stopped spinning. "This is a first for me," he said. "I've never been down here before, not all the way down on the floor of this crater. You can see how the lava flowed all over the place when it erupted the last time, and after that it got hard. I mean, down here the lava's almost like concrete. So let's go. We'll hike over to the cinder cone and climb up to the overlook."

"Forget that!" Jack barked. "I'm not letting you put my sister in danger by climbing that cinder cone. It probably isn't stable. We could get halfway up and slide back and we couldn't stop ourselves and we'd get cut to ribbons on the sharp volcanic cinders."

Jack felt ferocious; he must have looked that way too, because Danny meekly answered, "OK. Whatever you say, Jack."

Expecting an argument from Danny, Jack was momentarily at a loss for words. To give himself time to think, he checked his camera. It seemed fine, having survived the slippery slope in better shape than Jack had.

"So what'll we do?" Ashley asked him.

Jack did a slow 360-degree turn, trying to figure out just where they were and what options they had.

It was as if they were in a huge bowl of solidified black pudding, where all the froth had floated to the sides of the bowl and stuck there. The floor of Kilauea Iki Crater was flat, except in a few places where car-size blocks of lava had frozen in the lava lake when it cooled.

Where they were, the surface was jagged, sharp, and rough. But most of the crater floor looked smoother, like just-poured-out, charcoal-colored batter.

From where they stood, a path led in a nearly straight line all the way across the crater. It appeared to have been swept clean of cinders, probably by the boot soles of hikers who'd trekked that way, season after season.

"There's a trail," Jack announced, pointing at it.

"Right," Danny agreed.

"Where does it go?"

"To the other side of the crater, then up the bank."

"You mean *up* the bank like we just came *down* the bank?"

Danny laughed. "It's a real trail over there, Jack. It ends up close to Thurston Lava Tube." He laughed again. "You know what? There's a switchback trail over here, too, where we just came down. We could have taken it, but the way we did it was a lot faster. And more fun."

"Yeah. Fun." Shortcutting switchbacks was a major violation of park rules, and Danny probably knew that. One more reason to drop him into hot lava as soon as Jack could find some. But for now, he had to get both these kids back to his dad.

The trail across Kilauea Iki Crater looked safe enough. If it hadn't been, park rangers would have posted it with warning signs. But wait a minute. On closer examination, Jack noticed steam rising in different places on the crater floor. Because he'd visited Yellowstone National

Park a lot, Jack knew about steam vents. Here in Kilauea Iki Crater, the rain that had been falling—now slowed to a fine drizzle—must have drained down through cracks in the lava. There it got heated by the 2,000 degree magma far underground. When the rainwater grew hot enough, it drifted up again in the form of steam. Just like in Yellowstone.

"I'm still thinking," he announced. "Is there a parking lot over there where we can maybe find a ranger and hitch a ride to meet my dad?"

"Yep."

"You're sure, Danny?"

"Yep."

"How far is it across this crater?"

"About a mile. And flat most of the way till you come to the edge."

After a moment, Ashley asked impatiently, "Haven't you thought enough yet, Jack?"

"Yeah." He'd made up his mind. "We'll go across here and up the other side. But stay away from the steam vents, because if you get too close you could get burned. Or you could even fall down into the cracks, which would be a whole lot worse."

"I'm glad you finally figured it out, Jack," Danny told him, his voice rising with excitement. "Turn around."

"Why?" Jack asked. He was in no mood to

deal with any more of Danny's games.

"Just look behind you. Here comes the lady in the red shirt. I can see her tramping down the switchback trail, and she looks madder than ever."

Without another word, Danny took off, running across the crater.

6

Maybe she really was Pele, because whenever the woman appeared, nature began to act in peculiar ways. Right at that moment thunder roared like a cannon above their heads. That wasn't so different, because thunder had been booming for the past half hour. But now, mist began to rise, too, coming out of nowhere to shroud Kilauea Iki Crater in thin, cloudlike vapor.

It swirled around the woman but never entirely hid her flowing red tunic. Her strange words rang once more through the air.

"I told you she's Pele," Ashley declared and made a dash after Danny.

Stay. Face her. Find out what she wants, Jack told himself. There's no such thing as Pele. But as

From the condo's balcony, Steven, Ashley, and Jack looked straight out at the Pacific, all the way to the horizon.

A large, dark shape slid through the water not five feet ahead of him....

The other nēnē watched,
bright black eyes peering
out of a black face.

The ʻōhelo berries looked
like tiny, shiny red apples,
but waxy, and squashable.

Without another word,
Danny took off, running
across the crater.

"Pele's really cooking tonight!"

the mysterious woman got closer, she looked more frightening. Her hair stood out in a black cloud that seemed to puff up thicker, wider, and wilder, as if it had a life of its own. Though she was still several hundred feet away from Jack, he could read her expression clearly—fury!

Stand fast? Or run? As her shouts rose louder, adrenaline nudged him into fight-or-flight mode. He chose flight.

It wasn't that he was scared, he told himself. He had to look after Ashley and Danny and make sure they didn't get too close to the steaming fissures, those cracks in the lava crust. That became harder and harder to do as the mist rolled in, obscuring the trail.

"Wait, you guys!" he yelled. "Don't get off the trail." Did they hear him? He wasn't sure. The world around him was turning into a dream-scape—or worse, a nightmare of dimly seen shapes, dark and grotesque.

When he reached the biggest lava slabs and had to clamber over them, Jack realized he'd somehow missed the trail and was off to the side. "Ashley!" he yelled as loud as he could.

"Over here, Jack." She was teetering on top of one of the lava rocks just ahead of him. "Danny's right in front of me."

"Don't move till I come and get you," he yelled. "We've got to find the trail again. If we don't, we might fall into the fissures and get burned."

"Where's Pele?"

Jack was too charged up to argue with Ashley about who the woman was, Pele or not. "Last I saw her, she'd made it to the crater floor. Can't see her now. The mist is too thick."

Ashley slid down the lava block and landed at Jack's feet, saying, "I can hear her, though. Her footsteps. She's running. Come on Jack, we've got to get out of here!"

"I know, but I think she's pretty far behind us. This place is like a great big amphitheater," he said. "With these acoustics, you can't tell exactly where the footsteps are coming from. Danny," he yelled, "get over here beside me. We need to stay together so we don't get lost in this mist."

"Pele's making the steam rise," Danny told them, coming toward them through the fog like an apparition. "I've never seen it mist up this fast before. It's hard to tell the steam vents from the mist."

"It's like when we were in the airplane and we flew through clouds," Ashley said. "Jack, I still hear her coming. She's getting closer."

Jack grabbed both of them by their arms. "Listen to me. We gotta stay together so we can see each other. First we need to find the trail and get back on it, because that's the only place we know is for sure safe."

"Safe from her? Nuh-uh," Ashley said. "She'll

be following the same trail, right after us."

"Maybe, but the steam vents could hurt us worse than the woman can." That might not be true, Jack thought. With his own words of caution echoing in his ears, he felt uncertain and scared. Not so much of the steam vents, but of the woman. Worried about why she was chasing them. He turned and tried to locate her again, peering through curtains of mist that wafted like lengths of thin gauze blowing in a breeze.

Vapor swirled around him, hiding any trace of the woman. He was able to make out some of the outlines of the crater, its dark rim thrusting upward toward the sky, but even that lasted only briefly. The slabs and mounds of lava got swallowed by each new veil of fog that drifted across. He kept blinking his eyes as if that would clear his vision; it didn't help. He was lost in a featureless world.

"Let's go," he told them.

His voice sounded clear and strong, concealing the uncertainty he felt inside. "Stay together. We don't want to get separated in this soup."

He felt rather than saw a huge presence off to one side, but it was only the dark mound of the Puu Puai cinder cone, looming high above them. At its top, his dad was supposed to be waiting. Maybe Steven had left by now, to search Devastation Trail and the parking lot, trying to find his lost children. Was it as misty up there as down below?

"Puu Puai's on the right," Ashley said. "So the trail's to our left. Let go of my arm, Jack."

"Over here," Danny called out from the mist. "I found it."

How had he disappeared from Jack's careful watch? Jack had been certain he had both younger kids near him, right next to him, in fact. But somehow Danny had faded into the mist like a spirit.

A thought stabbed Jack's mind: If he couldn't see Danny, even when he was close by, then the woman could just as easily be close by, too, hidden by the vapor.

"Shhh," he commanded Ashley. "Stop and listen."

Both of them became perfectly still once again. There were no footsteps. No sound at all. They were safe. For now. "I think we lost her," Jack breathed. "Let's grab Danny and get out of here."

"Keep talking, Danny," Ashley called out, "so we can follow your voice."

"I scraped my leg crawling over a lava rock, but I don't think it's bleeding or anything. Long pants would have been better but my aunt Lan wanted me to wear these blue shorts because they go with this red, white, and blue shirt. She bought these for me just yesterday so I'd look nice when I met you, Jack. I mean, not just you, Jack, but your mom and dad and Ashley, too."

"Fine! You can shut up now. I see you."

Making sure he had Ashley by the hand, Jack hurried over to Danny.

Danny grabbed his other hand. "I heard something. Quiet!" he whispered.

Very clearly, they heard, once more, the crunch of footsteps.

"Oh, no! Pele's still here!" Ashley breathed.

Fear climbed from the pit of Jack's stomach into his mouth. He tried to swallow it down. Taking his sister by the shoulders, he made her face him. "Stop and think! Those footsteps are slow. She's having trouble seeing in this mist, just like we are. The Pele you keep talking about is a goddess. A goddess could see right through this pea soup and fly over to us and catch us. Whoever that is, it's just a human being and—"

"Who cares?" Danny said, yanking his hand free with so much force Jack's fingers stung.

"You stay with us!" Jack ordered.

"I will if you get moving."

"Puu Puai is still on our right, so we go straight ahead," Ashley told them quickly. "Run!"

"No, don't run. Just keep on the trail," Jack cautioned them.

They started out, moving fast, but as the mist grew more and more dense, they had to slow their steps.

Every few minutes they stopped to listen. The footsteps were always behind them, but—was it

Jack's imagination? They seemed to be getting a little more distant, the pacing more uncertain, the scuffing of cinders softer. They were losing her.

"Keep moving!" Jack ordered.

Every inch between them and their pursuer increased their safety, although what the actual danger was, Jack couldn't imagine. They pushed on, tripping on larger, baseball-size lava rocks strewn on the path, then righting themselves to move forward. The steps behind them faded into nothing.

"Hold it," Jack commanded.

Ashley and Danny froze in their tracks, with their mouths clamped shut to control even their breathing. It was deathly quiet.

"I don't hear her now," Ashley panted when she let out her breath. "How much farther to the end of this trail?"

"I can't tell," Danny answered. "It's too hard to see."

Holding up his hand, Jack strained once again to listen. There was no unworldly noise to break the stillness except the sound of his blood circulating against his eardrums. They'd made it. "She's gone!" he exclaimed, letting himself relax. "Nothing's going to hurt us now." The woman had fallen hopelessly behind them, lost in the mist. Jack had managed to keep Ashley and Danny and himself together.

And even though vapor hanging in the air obscured everything more than a few feet distant, Jack was certain they were still on the trail. He could look down and see its surface, so much smoother than the surrounding, hardened lava.

"Way to go, guys," Ashley said, although her lips still trembled. "Like Jack said, nothing can hurt us now."

"See, I told you she had to be a real person. Now do you—believe—she—was—just—a—woman?" As Jack spoke, something made his teeth click together, jarring his joints, shaking his insides. What was happening?

A deep rumbling spread beneath him. He felt suddenly disconnected, like a marionette being jerked by a hundred strings.

Ashley, her eyes wide, screamed, "Jack!"

"What is this?" Jack cried. He felt jostled like he was on an amusement park ride.

At the same instant Danny was shouting, "The ground's shaking. Oh-oh. Earthquake!"

The floor of the crater heaved up like a ripple in a carpet. Then it jerked sideways.

Danny yelled, "This one's big!"

"The b-book—" Ashley's voice was quavering. "It s-said Pele makes earthquakes by stamping her f-feet when she's mad!"

"Get down on the ground," Jack ordered. "Hang on!"

It seemed to go on forever, the rocking of the ground beneath them. Danny was flat on his belly, his head held up like a turtle's. Jack knelt on his hands and knees, head down, while Ashley lay on her side, rolled up in a ball, her hands grasping her ankles. None of them spoke a word, because the severe shaking drove every thought from their heads. There was nothing to hold onto—no trees, no walls, nothing except the earth itself, and the earth kept trying to shake them loose. Around them, big rocks were rolling down the crater walls.

Ashley moaned and clutched her stomach— any kind of motion always made her sick. Jack told her, "Don't throw up," but then he thought, what difference would it make if she did? They were out on a lava bed, not in someone's living room. As he had that thought—the first that had made any sense since the tremors started—he realized the shaking had slowed down some. In fact, a lot. Only a few little shudders remained.

He sat up, testing his tongue and lips to see whether they still worked since they'd gone dry from fright. "Is it over?" he asked.

"Yeah," Danny said, scrambling to his feet. "I bet that was about a six-point-oh on the Richter scale. There'll probably be some aftershocks."

"Aftershocks?" Ashley moaned.

"Don't worry, Ashley," Jack reassured her.

"We're through the worst now. We're OK."

"That's right," Danny told her. "Aftershocks usually aren't as bad as the first quake."

Jack stood up unsteadily, then went to where Ashley still lay curled, holding her stomach. Gingerly, one limb at a time, she unbent herself. Her skin was pale and waxy. She said, "I was scared, too, but mostly I was sick to my stomach." The clammy touch of her hand let Jack know how nauseated she'd felt.

"Better now?" he asked her. "We can handle a couple of aftershocks. They're no big deal. Right, Danny?"

Danny hesitated for just a moment before he answered, "Right."

Jack blinked hard. "Danny—is there something more?"

"No. Except maybe...."

"Except what? *What?*"

"It's just that sometimes, when there's a big earthquake around here, the volcano erupts, too."

Even in the dimness, Jack could see fear well in Ashley's eyes. "How soon?" she asked, her voice trembling. "Does the volcano come right away?"

"No. Usually it takes a couple of hours. And it probably won't be right here in Kilauea Iki Crater. I mean, I'm almost positive it won't be here. This exact spot hasn't had a really big eruption since 1959. Still, you never know."

Nervously, Jack brushed his palms against his shorts and said, "OK." He took another breath. "Just to make sure, we're going to get out of this crater as fast as possible."

"I'd say it's about a thousand to one it won't erupt here," Danny kept chattering. "All we really have to worry about are the aftershocks. But they won't be as bad. Volcano earthquakes like the ones here in Hawaii are different from earthquakes in places like California. Those happen from shifts in tectonic plates, but volcano earthquakes—"

"Danny!" Jack barked.

"What?"

"Shut up." The jolting from the quake hadn't done a thing to shut off Danny's mouth.

"I was just going to say that Kilauea earthquakes usually don't hurt anyone. Almost never. At least till the lava starts."

"So we'll get fried instead of scrambled," Jack said irritably.

Danny looked stricken. "Don't be mad at me, Jack."

"I'm not mad. We just don't have time to talk. Between aftershocks and even a thousand to one chance of lava right here on this spot, we need to get out of here." The mist seemed to have cleared a little more as they started down the trail again.

"And Pele's still behind us," Ashley worried. "She could catch up."

"Will you stop calling her Pele?" Jack demanded. He hadn't calmed down since the earthquake, and everything Danny or Ashley said seemed to touch a raw nerve. He felt responsible for both of them, but trying to keep them under control was like trying to organize hummingbirds in a box.

The mist ahead of them had broken up enough that they could easily see the trail now, but when Jack turned around to look behind him, the cloudy vapor back there was as thick as ever. And then he heard it. Far away, almost as if it were the scratching of a bird on gravel. Then louder, sharper. Footsteps. How could the woman have closed the gap between them so fast? They could hear her picking up speed.

The stomping of her feet grew louder.

"Not again! She's back!" Ashley cried.

"Go!" Jack yelled, and the three of them began to run.

The earthquake, although it lasted less than a minute, had seemed like an hour. Now their race through the crater—and they'd only been in Kilauea Iki Crater for about a half hour, according to Jack's watch—seemed to be in slow motion, as though they were running through a dream and their destination kept moving beyond reach.

The sound of their footsteps crunching on the lava was eerie enough. Add to that the mist, the earthquake, and the woman following them, and Jack wished all of it would really turn out to be nothing more than a bad dream, and he'd wake up soon in his bed in Jackson Hole, Wyoming.

At last Danny cried out, "I see trees over there. We're at the east wall. See it? We gotta climb it."

"Up the side?" Jack asked.

"It's rain forest up there. Real thick, so she won't see us. We could make it. I have this good sense of direction—"

"Oh, sure!" Jack exclaimed. "Your famous sense of direction got us into this."

"Give me another chance!"

What is with this kid? Jack thought. All this disaster is his fault, and we're still supposed to follow him?

"Let's do it," Ashley said. She was shivering. The sun had been hidden so long that the temperature had dropped, and all of them were wet, including their shoes. "I want to get out of here. I want to find Dad."

The closer they got, the higher the crater wall loomed over them. "That is one steep climb," Jack said. He was tired, he was wet, and he had to admit it—he was pretty scared. His heart thudded against his ribs, both from fear and from exertion. He knew how frightened Ashley was, too. Only Danny acted as if the whole chase were nothing more than a game, a chance for him to show off all the things he knew. As they climbed higher into the thick, ferny trees, Jack began to think he was crazy to have listened to Danny one more time.

"You said there was a trail," he told Danny.

"That woman'll take the trail. To lose her, we should go straight up the side."

If the ledge into the crater had been steep, this one was even steeper.

A cleared trail would certainly have been faster than battling through this dense greenery; they kept having to skirt around growth that was almost impassable. Even a machete wouldn't have done much good in the tangle of trees, roots, and ferns. And if they'd been wet before, by now they were absolutely dripping. Not only did drops fall down on them from the trees; the air was so humid Jack felt choked.

It was like swimming underwater.

His hair was plastered against his forehead. Ashley's dark hair, naturally wavy, had frizzed out sideways, except where the damp curls stuck to her neck. The careful, razor-straight part in Danny's hair had long since disappeared; now his head was covered with short, black spikes. What a mess they were. Steven would probably freak out when he saw them.

Jack felt for his camera, still under his shirt. He'd turned it backward so the lens was against his skin to protect it from moisture, but since the drops were running down his chest inside his shirt, his camera might be in trouble. No wonder they called this place a rain forest.

It was a struggle that wouldn't end. Bits of leaves stuck to their skin; the ground cover was slippery; all of them fell at least once and had to scramble up again. Ashley had a streak of grime across her cheek. As Jack checked his watch, he saw that his own hands were smeared with dirt. They'd been climbing for more than 20 minutes now. All of it straight up.

"OK, we're almost over the top," Danny called out. "Thurston Lava Tube is straight ahead, I think."

Puffing, Jack gave Ashley one last boost from behind. They cleared the ledge and emerged at the bottom end of a big parking lot. Danny stood waiting for them, poised like a runner listening for the starting gun to go off.

He pointed toward the upper part of the parking area, where someone was hurrying down the road in a quick, determined stride.

Right toward them.

The lady in red.

7

Where's a ranger?" Ashley cried. "You said there'd be rangers in the parking lot, Jack."

"Who cares?" Danny yelled. "Pele's coming fast. So let's split!" As usual, he ran off without bothering to check whether Jack or Ashley were following.

Unlike Danny, Ashley didn't dart across the road—she looked both ways to scout for traffic before she crossed. "What happened to all the people?" she called back to Jack. "There's no one around. Not even any cars."

"Yeah, it's deserted. The earthquake must have scared everyone away," he answered.

As they ran up an incline, Danny was so far ahead of them that the sound of his footsteps got drowned out by the pounding of their own. "Now where's he taking us?" Ashley wondered.

"To the lava tube," Jack puffed. "I saw the sign. That's where this path goes."

Ashley skidded to a halt. "Lava tube. Isn't that like a tunnel? I don't want to get stuck in a tunnel with Pele!"

"Ashley, we have to get Danny. If he hadn't run like he did, I would have stayed and asked the woman what she's after. I'm getting sick of running."

"I'm not," Ashley said.

The paved path cut through the middle of a fern forest, the most intense green Jack had ever seen outside of a jar of poster paint. Some of the trees had aerial roots dangling down from their branches; they looked like the tentacles of jellyfish. Others trees bloomed with spiky red blossoms. On the way up from the crater, Danny had said they were 'ohi'a trees.

The tall tree ferns were the most numerous. Their trunks curled at the tips with embryonic fronds as tightly coiled as snail shells; eventually, they would unfurl and grow large. Jack thought they looked creepy, like something from the movie *Alien*. The forest's silence made things even creepier. He heard bird calls, but no human sound.

When they got close to Thurston Lava Tube, metal handrails edged the path on both sides, hemming them in. Rough rocks surrounded the face of the tube, with more ferns and beardlike moss hanging down around the entrance like a drooping, green mustache.

Again Ashley hesitated. "Do we have to go in there?"

"You're the one who's not sick of running."

"I know, but molten lava once flowed through that tube, right?"

"Right."

"Danny says there's going to be another lava eruption pretty soon because of the earthquake."

"Danny doesn't know everything."

"What if we get inside and an eruption starts and the lava pours through and we get melted?"

"That's not going to happen, Ashley."

"But what if it does?"

"Then we'll be liquefied and you won't have to worry about the woman in red. Now start moving. Danny's way ahead of us."

Cautiously, one hesitant step after another, Ashley slipped through the mouth of the tube. "It's gonna be real dark in here, isn't it?"

"They've got lights along the wall. Come on! You're such a wimp." Satisfied that Ashley was right behind him—he was certain of it, because she was hanging onto the back of his shirt—Jack raised his head and yelled, "Danny!"

His voice echoed weirdly. The lava tube yawned in front of them, a 12-foot-high artery into the heart of the earth. Every 20 feet or so, lights had been placed halfway up the walls. Glow from the lamps reflected on the rough surfaces, turning them the color of brass.

"I'm here," Danny yelled back.

"Where? I can't see you."

"Keep coming. Is the red lady following us?"

"No. She quit. So come on back."

"Nuh-uh. You come here."

"Fine," Jack muttered to Ashley. "We'll have to go out the other end. At least the tube isn't very long...I don't think."

"Why can't he come to us?" she asked. "Come on, Danny," she shouted. "Let's go out the front entrance. We're not too far in here yet; I can still see daylight at the mouth of the tunnel."

"No. My way's better."

Jack didn't bother to answer.

He suddenly realized he was tired. Brain-crushingly tired of Pele and lava and earthquakes. Tired of being responsible. All he wanted now was to find his dad and let him worry about all the things—mainly Danny—that Jack could not control.

Since they'd begun their hike, Jack had made it his job to keep them all together, to think things through and protect them from the frightening bursts of nature and the mysterious, strange woman.

The mental game of cat and mouse had wiped him out.

There were no answers, just questions. Now all he could think about was getting out the other side of the tunnel and ending the chase, once and for all. After they'd walked a little distance, Ashley complained, "It sure is wet in here."

"What's the difference? We're already soaked." Overhead, a few small lava stalactites hung from the roof of the cave like icicles, dripping water into thin puddles on the floor. Everywhere they went in Hawaii, it seemed, they got rained on or dripped on or misted from vapor, not to mention soaking in the ocean on the first two days, but that part was voluntary. He began to appreciate the dry climate of his own native Wyoming. There, if you got wet, you dried out fast. Here, you stayed wet.

Looking back, he saw that the light beyond the cave's entrance had shrunk from a capital O to a small o to a dot and then disappeared. He squinted to see ahead of him, because the tube wasn't supposed to be all that long and maybe he'd be able to glimpse the light outside the cave's exit. But he couldn't. They must be right in the middle of Thurston Lava Tube, shut off from all natural light.

Step, step, step, pulling Ashley along.

Then the tingling started underfoot.

"Oh-oh! The cave's moving!" she yelled.

"Aftershock!" Jack exclaimed. "Not a real earth-quake. Not as bad." Even as he said that his voice cracked and his stomach clamped with fear. As he crouched on the cave floor beside his sister, his mind shot into high gear and he imagined all the things that could happen.

Some of the sharp stalactites could break off from the shaking and fall straight down on their heads like little knives. It could be a volcano erupting, and hot lava could stream into the tube and burn them up. No, that was too farfetched. But if this turned out to be a real earthquake even stronger than the last one, the roof of the lava tube could collapse on them and bury them alive. Oh man!

Again, there was nothing to hang onto except the ground. With his palms flat against the floor of the lava tube, Jack could feel every vibration.

Fortunately, the shaking stopped pretty quickly. It was an aftershock, after all.

Jack blew a slow breath between his teeth. They'd made it. Again.

"I hate earthquakes!" Ashley exclaimed. "But I didn't feel as sick in the stomach this time."

She sounded calmer than Jack expected, calmer than he felt.

"Danny," Jack called out. "Are you OK?"

"I'm fine," he called back. "I told you I'm tough. And that one was probably only a four-point-oh."

"Don't go anywhere," Jack ordered. "I want to get you, get out of this place, and find my dad." He was just about to tell Ashley to start walking again when, all at once, the lights went out.

They were surrounded by inky blackness, without a splinter of light.

"Jack!" Ashley wailed. "What happened? I can't see!"

"I guess the aftershock knocked out the electric p-power," Jack stammered. Never in his life had he experienced such total darkness. Even the times he worked in the photography darkroom with his father, there was always a small amount of light so they could see what they were doing. Here, he couldn't even find his hand in front of his face.

"Whooo. This is wild!" Danny's yell reached them from who knew how far away in the tunnel.

"We'll just stay put till the lights come back on," Jack shouted. "It'll probably be quick."

"Maybe not," Danny called back. "Last week when the power was down, it took hours to fix."

"Oh great!" Ashley groaned.

Jack yelled, "We'll give it a few minutes. If it doesn't come back on, then we'll just have to feel our way out."

"Oh, great!" Ashley repeated. "Really, really great!"

"Well, what else are we gonna do? Stay here all day?" Jack wished he had the kind of watch that lit up in the dark. Minutes dragged; the only sound was water dripping from the ceiling.

It would have been easier if Jack had known exactly how much time was passing.

Even talkative Danny, wherever he was, stayed quiet as the blackness pressed down on them. It seemed to Jack that the whole day had fallen into a black hole, where time crystallized around him, hard and immovable, and he could never come out the other side.

After a while he could no longer stand the waiting. "Come on, let's go," he told Ashley.

"In the dark?"

"We'll feel our way along the wall. We can go real slow. I'll go first; you stay right behind me."

The blind leading the blind, Jack thought as they shuffled at a snail's pace along the wet, uneven cave floor, with Ashley holding onto Jack's shoulder from behind.

He hoped they were heading in the right direction—he might have gotten turned around in the dark. Still, either direction would eventually get them out of the tube. But what if there was a big hole ahead and he tripped in it and broke an ankle or something?

He was just about to tell Ashley that maybe this wasn't such a great idea after all and they should stop fumbling around and just wait, when she clutched his shoulder hard.

"Do you hear it?" she gasped.

"What?"

"Footsteps. Ohmygosh! She's here!"

Jack strained to listen. Ashley was right. Someone was walking through the lava tube, in the dark, coming toward them. The steps were loud, purposeful, with a steady beat as even as a metronome, and getting nearer. The game wasn't over. She was here. She was back.

There was no mistaking those footfalls: a very large person was approaching.

Slow, heavy steps sounded in the blackness, unhurried and deliberate.

The dark wasn't stopping her.

For an instant Jack couldn't push his fear away enough to make a plan. Even if that—presence— behind them could see in the dark, he couldn't.

"She's coming!" Ashley cried.

"Come on!" Jack ordered.

He pulled his camera out of his shirt and told Ashley, "Get ready to run. I'm going to fire off the flash. It'll light the lava tube for a second. Run as far as you can see."

It was just a little point-and-shoot camera with a flash only strong enough for close-ups, but in total darkness any light would seem bright. "Ready, go!" He pushed the button, praying that his batteries had enough juice, that the dampness hadn't shorted out the camera's electrical system.

It worked. The flash dazzled their eyes, but the brief flare of light gave them a glimpse of where to run. He fired it again until Ashley screamed.

"What?" he yelled.

"Something's got me!" she shrieked, stopping dead. "It's grabbing my hair!"

Jack's hands started to shake.

Pointing the camera toward the roof of the cave, he hit the flash again. In the momentary burst of light, he could see the stringlike tendrils dangling toward them.

"They're roots," Ashley gasped.

"Growing down from above. Come on," he said, and fired off the flash again.

Danny's voice drifted back, bouncing off the walls of the cave. "What are you doing? That light's blinding me."

"Turn around and run," Jack shouted. "The lady's back."

Eight, nine, ten times he hit the button and the camera's flash kept firing. Work, work! he begged it. Eleven, twelve times, and ahead of them they saw daylight. "Yes! There's the exit," Jack shouted.

Out the opening they ran, up a flight of steps and right into the arms of a park ranger.

"Hey, what's your hurry?" she asked.

"Someone's chasing us," all three of them answered. "The lady in red—"

"She's been after us since Kilauea Iki—"

"Slow down," the ranger began. "You're all talking at once."

"She's still in the lava tube. Listen, you can hear her coming!"

"Yeah, her footsteps."

"Who is she?" the ranger asked.

"We don't know! A stranger we never saw before."

The ranger ran down the steps and pointed her flashlight into the yawning darkness of the lava tube. "I don't see anyone. I don't hear anyone, either," she said. "Are you sure you're telling me the truth? You're not just making this up?"

"Honest, she's in there." All three of them were chattering at once because finally there was someone to listen to them, to help them.

Slowly, the ranger came back up the steps and stood in front of them.

She wore the standard National Park Service uniform: gray shirt with the logo on the sleeve, and dark green pants. Her name badge said Tricia Milewski. Her copper-colored hair probably would have blazed in the sun if there'd been any sunlight overhead.

She stared at them, one after the other.

"I swear we are telling the truth!" Ashley cried, raising her right hand. With the fright that glinted in Ashley's dark eyes, no one could possibly doubt her, Jack thought.

"OK." From a leather case hanging on her belt, the ranger took out a two-way radio and spoke into it.

"Better get a few people over here," she said. "I've got three kids here who say they've been chased by a stranger. In Thurston Lava Tube. And they say she was stalking them even before that. Yes, a woman. They called her, uh, 'the lady in red.'"

When she reported that part, Ranger Milewski raised her eyebrows as though she still wasn't too sure about all this, and was a little embarrassed telling the story to the park's central dispatcher.

"Please," Jack said, touching her sleeve, "have someone call our mom. I'm Jack Landon and this is my sister, Ashley, and that's Danny Tran. Our mother is with a biologist named Darcy over at the research center—"

"Whoa. Slow down!" the ranger said once more, and held up her hand. "Now tell me again. Your name's—?"

"Jack Landon. Ashley Landon." He pointed. "Danny Tran. Our mom's at the research center with a biologist named Darcy."

"Well, actually," Danny broke in, "she isn't my

mother, she's their mother. My mother's dead. Theirs isn't."

Again, Tricia stared at them as though she couldn't believe all this was for real. "What?" she asked into the radio. "He is? OK. Connect me." She cupped her hand over the two-way radio and told them, "Another ranger has been guarding the entrance to the tube ever since the lights went out. No one's been allowed inside—" She paused briefly. "Yeah, Keith? Did anyone go into the lava tube since you've been at the entrance? No? There's three kids here who say a woman chased them."

Tricia listened for a moment, then carefully put the radio back into its case. "If what you kids are saying is true," she began, "then the woman is still in there. I've called for backup. When they get here, one ranger will go through the front entrance and another will enter the cave through this back opening. The woman who was chasing you won't be able to escape. They'll find her and bring her out."

8

Let us through, please!" Two grim-looking rangers, a man and a woman, clambered down the stairs to the back opening of Thurston Lava Tube. But instead of guns in their hands, they carried long-handled flashlights.

Jack felt like he was in the middle of a television drama.

After the rangers disappeared into the cavern, Tricia told Jack and Ashley, "We've contacted your mother at the research center, and your father, too—he was at park headquarters, asking for help to find you." She tossed back her coppery hair as she added, "So! We're going to meet both of them at the Hawaiian Volcano Observatory. We can leave right now. My car's parked across the road."

"No!" Ashley said.

"No?"

"I'm not going till they bring her out."

"The woman in red," Danny added, as if anyone might not know who they were talking about.

"Are you sure you want to see her?" Tricia began, looking doubtful.

"Positive." Now that they were on the other side of the lava tube, the fear had melted from Ashley's eyes. In its place was determination. She was ready to confront her tormentor, and Jack realized that he was, too.

After all that chasing, all that threatening, they all needed to get a good, close look at this woman and discover just who she was.

"OK, then," Tricia said. "Two other rangers have gone into the front entrance to search the tube from that end. I'll radio them to bring her out this way."

They could hear the talk, staticky and muffled, crackling over the two-way radio in Tricia's hand:

You see anything?

No, do you?

No. Gotta check it out, though. Someone threatening kids—

Tricia glanced at Jack, Ashley, and Danny, and shook her head. Jack didn't know how to interpret the headshake. Did it mean the rangers couldn't find the woman, or did it mean they were doubting the kids' story? Or maybe it just meant let's wait and see what turns up here. He stood unmoving with Danny and Ashley, all of them silent and breathing softly, their attention riveted on the radio in Tricia's hand.

How far are you guys?

About halfway. Hey! The lights are back on.

Good! That makes it easier.

"They can finish searching a lot quicker now that the lights are back," Tricia said. "It'll only take them about ten minutes to search the tube thoroughly."

It was almost as if Jack could feel the digital seconds ticking away on his wrist.

Then one single voice came over the two-way radio: *Tricia, there's no one in here except us. We're gonna need to talk to those kids.*

"Got it," Tricia answered. Jack's stomach sank.

Ashley's eyes had grown huge. "We heard her footsteps! If they can't find her, then—"

"Then what?" Tricia asked.

"It must have been Pele."

Watching Tricia's face, Jack was sure he saw a flicker of—what was it? Not surprise. And it wasn't anything like doubt. Maybe just the opposite— a split-second look of belief. But it was gone so fast, and her expression returned to normal so quickly, that Jack wasn't sure just what he'd seen. If anything.

Tricia leaned forward to be at eye level with Ashley. "I understand what you might be thinking," she said. "In this place, with all the fire and ashes and burned-out desolation, it's easy to think you've seen Pele. When you see lava flowing, and you hear the native Hawaiians chanting about Pele and dancing in her honor—well, I've felt her presence myself, in a way. But listen, Ashley—"

Tricia leaned even closer. "I've got to fill out a report. If I write down that Pele was chasing you, my bosses aren't going to take it too seriously."

Tricia straightened. "You've pretty much convinced me that you kids saw *someone*—"

"We did," Jack said emphatically. "It was a real person. My sister just...believes in things. Please don't put down what she said."

"I won't."

Jack kept insisting, almost starting to prattle because he felt he had to convince this ranger in front of him, "There was an actual woman chasing us, honest! I promise you. We saw her and we heard her. Right, Danny?"

For once, Danny, the motormouth, stayed quiet. He glanced from Jack to Ashley to Tricia, and after that he stared at the ground.

Finally, he spoke. "I've lived here for three years," he said. "I've heard lots of stories."

"All of us have," Tricia answered gently. "You can't stay around Kilauea without hearing... about things."

What was going on here? Was Jack the only

person hooked into reality? Just then the four tall rangers came out of the lava tube and surrounded the kids.

"Want to tell us again what happened?" the tallest one asked quietly. "Let's go over it once more about what you think you saw."

"Never mind. I've got it all up here," Tricia said, tapping her forehead. "They've been talking to me. Now we need to take them back to their parents. We'll get everything straightened out at the Hawaiian Volcano Observatory. You guys come, too, if you want."

The three men and one woman who had done the search took time to consider what to do. While the discussion went on, circling around the group, Ashley slipped her hand into Jack's and held on hard.

"Maybe you can handle it without us, Tricia," one of the rangers said. "We've got other things going—the seismologists say there may be an eruption pretty soon. We need to start evacuating hikers and closing some of the roads. Would you leave a copy of your report in my box, though?"

At the word "eruption," Danny's face got its "I-told-you-so" look.

When they climbed out of Tricia's car at the Hawaiian Volcano Observatory parking lot, two nēnē waddled up to them, their heads held forward as they came.

"Little beggars," Tricia said. "That's how these geese get into trouble. They come along looking for handouts, and people feed them. Then they associate cars and people with food, so they walk out onto roads and end up getting run over."

"Is it illegal to feed them?" Jack asked.

"You bet! If a ranger saw you feeding one you'd be in big trouble."

Jack wondered how much trouble they were already in, since they'd reported being chased by a woman who seemed to have vanished. Calling out a bunch of park rangers on a wild-goose chase was probably a worse offense than feeding real, live wild geese.

"Come on, we'll go inside and see if your mom and dad are here yet," Tricia said. "You won't be allowed into the actual observatory, where the geologists are at work, but you can wait inside the museum. It's right next door."

The Thomas A. Jaggar Museum was a long but low stone building with windows all around.

Since Olivia and Steven hadn't yet arrived, Tricia invited the kids to explore the place.

What caught Jack's eye first was a globe of the Earth, and beside it, another Earth globe with a section carved out to reveal fire at the planet's core. A sign said that magma/lava comes from

Earth's mantle, just under the oceanic crust.

Hands clasped behind his back, Danny stood beside Jack to examine the display, while Ashley moved along the wall looking at murals.

"Jack!" she yelled. Her voice echoed in the hushed room. "Look at this!"

"Just a second, Ashley. I want to see this globe."

"But...it's her!"

Ashley was staring wide-eyed at the wall. When they reached her, Jack and Danny saw a mural of a brown-skinned woman with blazing eyes, with ropes of black lava for hair, and a wreath of red blossoms circling her head.

"That's the woman who chased us! Isn't it, Jack? Isn't it, Danny?"

Tricia had come quickly to stand next to Ashley. She put her hand on Ashley's shoulder and said, "That's a painting of Pele. I mean, that's how this particular artist thought Pele would look. Other artists paint her differently."

"But it's just like she really looked," Ashley insisted. "It's the woman who chased us."

Another woman ranger, who couldn't have known anything about why Jack and Danny and Ashley were there, drifted over toward them and said, "Those blossoms in her hair are called lehua. They're sacred to Pele, probably because they're red. Red is Pele's color."

The woman's name tag said Matilda Wong; that was a Chinese name. People from lots of different backgrounds lived in Hawaii, Jack had noticed. Matilda Wong's hair was black and straight, like Danny's, but hers was perfectly groomed, while Danny's had become matted and messy. Danny and Ashley both looked like refugees from a war zone. Jack guessed he did too.

Ranger Wong smiled at Ashley, mistaking her wide-eyed, half-frightened look for interest. Continuing with her talk, which she probably gave to visitors dozens of times a day, she said, "'Ōhelo berries are sacred to Pele, too. You're not supposed to eat them until you offer the first ones you pick to Pele."

"Offer them?" Ashley asked, her voice trembling a little. "Offer them how?"

"Come with me," the woman said, taking Ashley by the hand. "I'll show you. You can come, too," she said, gesturing to Jack and Danny. Tricia said nothing, but trailed along behind them.

"Over there," Ranger Wong told them. "That's Halemaumau Crater. That's Pele's home."

The observatory and museum were perched on the west rim of Kilauea Caldera—a crater so huge it dwarfed Kilauea Iki. Looking down, they saw that one part of the caldera held a pit crater—an even deeper hole inside the wide, already deep hole of the caldera. Steam rose white against the dark, barren floor of the crater.

"Halemaumau Crater, is where Pele lives," the ranger went on. "The sacred fire pit. Before you eat the 'ōhelo berries, you must throw the first few in the direction of Halemaumau, as a gift to Pele."

"What—?" Ashley's voice was a little hoarse now. "What happens if you don't?"

Still smiling, the ranger wagged a finger at them and said, "Then Pele gets very angry and causes mischief. In one of our interpretive books, it says that a missionary who came here from the mainland long, long ago, offended Pele by not offering her 'ōhelo berries before he ate them. Wait, let me get the book."

She was gone for less than a minute and came back holding a slim black booklet with the same picture of Pele on the cover as hung on the wall behind them. "Here," she said. "I'll read it to you in the very words of the missionary, Hiram Bingham. He wrote, 'a prophetess...calling herself Pele...approached...marching with a haughty step, with long, black dishevelled hair and countenance wild, with spear...in her hands....' Well, anyway, she confronted the missionary and she was pretty mad at him."

"What did she do to him?" Danny asked. "Did she stick the spear in him, or burn him with lava?"

"Oh, I don't think either of those things." The ranger laughed a little. "She just told him to leave Hawaii and go home."

"That's not so bad," Ashley said, looking relieved.

"But people who offend Pele often report that from then on, their lives change for the worse. Unhappy things happen to them," Matilda Wong said.

"Danny." Ashley turned accusing eyes and an accusing finger on him. "You didn't offer any berries to Pele before you ate them back there, when we were on Devastation Trail."

"Yeah, uh—well...."

Before Danny could answer further, Tricia announced, "I think these must be your parents coming through the door."

It was. "Mom!" Ashley cried, and she ran into Olivia's arms.

Steven strode across the room to give Jack and Danny quick hugs and then asked, "What happened to you? How did you get lost?"

"We took a wrong turn," Jack answered.

There was too much that needed saying to spill it all out right there and right then, in front of other people. Jack had to sort things out in his own head, to try to make sense of the mystery.

Or of any piece of it.

How much was true? How much superstition

or myth? What part of it was real and what part had been triggered by Ashley's imagination, making them hear things they couldn't really have heard, and see things that weren't there?

9

Jack was tired of it. He wanted all of it to stop.

At half past five, when they'd left the Jaggar Museum, his parents had decided they'd rather not make the three-hour drive all the way back to their condo on the western side of the island. They managed to get two rooms at Volcano House, the only hotel inside the park. At last Jack, Ashley, and Danny were able to clean up, dry off, and slip into the new Hawaii T-shirts they'd bought at the gift shop.

It was a nice hotel, perched right on the rim of Kilauea Caldera, with a great view and a lava-stone fireplace in the lobby.

It was said that the fire in the fireplace hadn't gone out in 125 years. Even when one of the earlier versions of the hotel burned down, embers from the fireplace were saved and carefully tended. Then, when Volcano House was rebuilt, the embers were moved once again into the fireplace, to blaze up in welcoming warmth.

Now the Landons, plus Danny, ringed a table in the hotel dining room. They were seated beside a big glass window where, if they wanted to, they could look right out at Kilauea Caldera. But no one was paying much attention to the view.

Jack heaved a sigh. From the time they'd sat down with menus in front of them, all the while they skimmed the menus and decided what to order, when they started on their salads and buttered their breadsticks, and clear up to this moment, halfway through the meal, they'd talked about only one thing.

The woman who'd chased them.

And Jack had had just about enough of it.

They'd discussed it from every angle, every possibility. "I still can't believe she was stalking you," Steven had said. "People just don't do that sort of thing right out in the open, where others can see them."

Steven always had trouble believing people could be mean or cruel, or even stupid. At least not on purpose. His view of human nature was that most folks were basically good and decent.

Olivia, though, declared, "I'd like to get my hands on that woman, whoever she was. How dare she frighten my children!"

Olivia, a wildlife biologist, was used to animal predation. She knew that certain animals could be sneaky as they stalked their victims and vicious when they caught them, and to her, humans at times behaved like that, too. Ashley had gone on and on with her ideas about Pele. And Danny, who thought a thousand words were better than any picture, expressed his own theories about what had happened that day, most of them directed to Jack.

And Jack wanted it to end.

To change the subject, he asked his mother, "How did it work out in your meeting with Darcy and the other scientists?"

"Very well. Darcy's got a lot of valuable data on the nēnē."

"Like what?" Jack asked, hoping to keep the conversation moving in that direction.

"Well, they're having trouble with feral cats."

"What are feral cats?" Ashley wanted to know.

"When people dump unwanted cats or kittens out on the highway, and they manage to live and breed in the wild, their offspring grow up untamed, or feral. Feral cats kill nēnē for food. So do mongooses."

Although he knew the answer, Jack asked, "What are mongooses?"

"I know, Jack." Danny actually raised his hand, like he was in a classroom. "They look like big rats but they're really civets. They were imported to the Hawaiian Islands to kill rats in the sugar-cane fields, but then they started spreading and now they're as much trouble as the rats."

"Right, Danny. And rats hurt the nēnē, too, because they're egg biters. They destroy the eggs," Olivia said.

"Boy, no wonder the poor nēnē have trouble surviving," Steven commented.

"Guess what?" Olivia said. "Predators aren't the big problem anymore. It's starvation."

"Starvation!" they all exclaimed.

"Uh-huh." Olivia looked from one to the other of them, pleased at their interest in the fate of the nēnē. She told them, "In the first year of life, from the time the goslings hatch until they're a year old, ninety percent of them die. Mainly from starvation. At least that's what Darcy thinks happens to them. Nine out of ten times, the goslings just vanish."

"Lots of things just vanish around here," Ashley said grimly. "Like, strange women vanish right out of lava tubes."

Jack shot his sister a look, then asked, "Why should they starve, Mom? We saw some nēnē today, and they looked nice and fat. They seemed to have plenty to eat."

Olivia put down her fork and laced her fingers, going into her earnest-lecture mode. She loved explaining things to anyone willing to listen. "You saw adult nēnē. They've adapted to the vast changes in the Hawaiian environment. But the goslings seem more restricted in their diet, and in some places they can't find enough nourishment. No one knows what the goslings are supposed to eat, what their natural diet was before humans came onto the islands and changed the ecological system."

"And killed nearly all of the nēnē," Danny added. "Like I said, once there were only about thirty of them left on all the Hawaiian Islands."

Olivia had become so intent on what she was saying, so eager to share it, that she forgot to pick up her fork again. "You've hit on another problem," she told Danny. "There are always lots of pieces to a puzzle. And one more piece to this one is genetic variability."

"Huh?" Even Danny didn't understand what that meant.

"You know how you get different characteristics from your parents and your other ancestors? If all your ancestors had exactly the same genes, then you'd be just like they were. Same color hair, same color eyes, same height—no diversity. No variability."

"What's wrong with that, Mom?" Jack asked.

"Well, say a plague came along and you had no defenses against it. You and all your relatives would be wiped out. But someone with a different mixture of genes might survive the plague. So they'd live and reproduce."

She took a sip of her water and continued, "Hawaii is very different today than it was before people came. When an environment changes, a variety of genetic combinations can help a species survive. But today's nēnē are all descended from only a handful of birds. If their species had more genetic diversity, they might be able to adapt better to the changes."

"I have lots of genetic diversity," Danny said. "Three-quarters Vietnamese and one-quarter American—that's me. And I'm a survivor."

"Right," Olivia said, smiling at him. "And you're strong, and smart, and you've already done a lot of adapting in your life."

"And I'm tough, too," Danny declared.

Sure you are, Jack thought. It was comical the way this little 65-pound weakling kept bragging about how tough he was.

Steven broke in, "What have you survived, Danny, besides possibly being chased by Pele?"

Danny seemed to freeze. He stared down at his plate, focusing on the pale blue scalloped pattern etched on the rim.

After a moment he answered, "Oh, the usual stuff. Measles, chicken pox—you know. I'm OK now."

Not taking her eyes from Danny's face, Ashley said, "I had the chicken pox, too. I hated it. I itched. But...." She took a breath, and Jack could see she had something more than chicken pox on her mind. "Danny, I've been wanting to ask you something since we were back on the trail. Remember that thing you said, about the helicopters—?"

The waiter came just then to ask if they were through with their dinners and whether they wanted any dessert.

Danny seemed grateful for the interruption, grilling the waiter about every dessert the restaurant had to offer.

The grownups ordered cappuccinos, Ashley chose chocolate pie, and Jack and Danny finally settled on banana splits.

"Mrs. Landon, is that the kind of work you do all the time? I mean, you always try to save animals?" Danny asked, looking at her intently.

She nodded. "And lots of other things, besides."

"That is so cool! I'd love to do stuff like that."

Now Olivia really smiled, turning her full, do-you-really-mean-it look of delight on Danny. "There's no reason on earth why you can't, some-day, Danny. When we get back to Jackson Hole, I'll take you with me to visit the elk refuge and the laboratory where I work."

Jack was somewhat surprised—he'd never

thought his mother's profession was all that exciting. Maybe he was just too used to what she did. He'd grown up around it, hearing about it each night at the dinner table. She fed elk, checked wildlife for disease, and ran tests on other species, like the nēnē, to explain their genetic makeup in wildlife journals.

To Jack, it was all ordinary, everyday stuff. It was just his mother's job.

His father's photography, now—that really excited him. In a couple more years, when he was old enough to get a part-time job, Jack wanted to save up for some good-quality camera equipment, the way his father was always saving to buy new lenses and darkroom supplies. The best equipment cost a lot, but it paid off in better pictures.

"Folks," the waiter said, setting hot cups of cappuccino in front of Steven and Olivia, "have you heard that a volcano is erupting?"

"See, Jack, what did I tell you?" Danny exclaimed. "I knew one would go off!"

"Where?" Steven asked.

"At Puu Oo. You won't want to miss it. Just drive about four miles down Chain of Craters Road to the Mauna Ulu parking area, then hike the trail about a mile to Puu Huluhulu. The eruption will still be five miles away from you, but don't worry, you'll see plenty. Oh, and don't forget your flashlights."

"Gotta run and grab my camera," Steven said, jumping up from the table. "I'll pick up some flashlights at the gift shop."

"Finish your cappuccino. It'll get cold," Olivia warned him.

"Hot lava's more important than hot java," he answered. "Be right back."

Olivia laughed. "He's absolutely right. You kids hurry and eat your dessert. We're in for a much bigger treat than chocolate pie."

What a wild ending to a wild day!

All the way over in the car, as daylight faded, they watched an orange glow tint the bottom of the clouds that hung in the sky above Puu Oo crater cone.

It was dark when they reached the parking area, but judging from the many jiggling flashlight beams they saw, dozens of people were hurrying down the trail.

Even before they rounded the last bend in the trail they heard a dull roar, like a jet plane taking off, followed by ooohs and ahhhs that rose from the watching crowd.

Then they saw it, too—a bright orange fountain of fire shooting up from Puu Oo crater cone, east of them.

Jack couldn't tear his eyes from the spectacle.

He'd seen lots of videotapes of volcanoes in

action, but pictures could never begin to reveal the eeriness of that glow against the night sky. He was so caught up in it that he jumped when he felt a hand on his shoulder.

For a couple of seconds he didn't recognize the woman behind him, but then he realized it was Tricia Milewski, the park ranger from Thurston Lava Tube. She looked different out of uniform, her copper hair tied back in a scrunchie, a green zipper jacket replacing her uniform shirt.

"Hi," she said. "How do you like our fireworks?"

"Better than Fourth of July," Jack answered. And it was.

These were nature's fireworks.

Compared with a pyrotechnic display like this one, anything humans could make was kindergarten stuff.

"There's better yet to come," Tricia told them as she peered through her binoculars. "Just wait. The crater's starting to overflow right now. Want to take a look?" she asked, handing Jack the binoculars.

Jack, Ashley, Danny, and Olivia took turns staring through the binoculars at the superheated lava rolling down the flanks of the cinder cone.

Steven was busy with his camera, so he got a magnified view, through his zoom lens, of the orange and black rivers of lava that began to descend the west slopes of Puu Oo like creeping fingers, moving slowly, but glowing brightly.

"Look at that!" Ashley exclaimed. "It's like melted chocolate, on fire."

They watched for an hour, feeling a sense of closeness to the dozens of awestruck, appreciative people surrounding them, as everyone marveled at the majestic sight of a volcano in action.

"Incredible!" some of them would cry out. Or, "Isn't that beautiful? Pele's really cooking tonight!"

Then Olivia noticed Ashley's teeth chattering. "Hey, you guys are getting cold," she said. "I think we better get you to bed."

After saying goodnight to Tricia and the other friendly watchers whose names they didn't even know, the Landons returned reluctantly to their car and to their rooms in Volcano House.

Jack and Danny shared one room with two beds in it; Ashley, Steven, and Olivia had a connecting room with a double bed and a pull-out sofa. They hadn't brought any extra clothes with them, so Jack and Ashley had to sleep in their T-shirts and underwear.

"You have all your luggage with you, Danny," Steven mentioned. "You can unpack whatever you usually sleep in so you'll be more comfortable."

"I want to be like Jack," Danny answered.

"OK. I'm going to close the door connecting our two rooms," Steven told them, "but if you need anything during the night, just wake me."

"Sure, Dad," Jack said. "I know how easy it is to wake you." Steven slept like a log. Nothing short of an alarm ringing in his ear ever dragged him out of a night's sleep.

"Well, wake your mother, then," Steven said, yawning. "Night, guys."

ack liked to spend his nights with a wide-open window letting in plenty of air, and in this hotel, luckily, you could open the windows. A breeze stirred the curtains, blowing them inward. Outside, a full moon hung in the sky. He turned on his side to face the window, enjoying the moon.

Suddenly a light blazed. Danny had switched on the table lamp between their beds.

"Why'd you do that?" Jack asked.

"I can't sleep. Too much happened today. Maybe we could talk for a while, Jack."

Jack nearly groaned out loud. All Danny had done all day was talk, talk, talk. Turning to face him, he asked, "What do you want to talk about?"

"I dunno. You pick a subject. I can talk about anything."

With the light on, the room was bright enough that Jack noticed the doorknob beginning to turn, slowly. An inch at a time, soundlessly, the door opened. Jack felt a pinch of alarm. He raised up on his elbow, staring. Danny, who'd already begun to talk and who was facing Jack, didn't see the door open wider, and wider, until—

"Ashley! Go back to bed," Jack shouted.

"Shhhh! I can't sleep."

Danny grabbed the blankets and pulled them up to his shoulders. "I'm in my underwear!" he cried.

"I won't look. There's something I want to talk about," she said.

"Great!" Jack rolled over to face the window again. "You and Danny can have a nice long yak fest. You deserve each other. I'm going to sleep."

"Fine! Sweet dreams, crab meat. Now, Danny," Ashley began, "I've come to a conclusion. I think you've been hiding something from us."

That sounded interesting, so Jack turned back to see what his sister was getting at. Ashley, wearing Steven's T-shirt, which hung down to her knees, had both hands on her hips.

"What do you mean?" Danny asked. He pulled the blankets up to his neck. "Hiding what?"

"I just have the feeling there's something you're not telling us."

Now the blankets were all the way up to

Danny's eyes. He peeked out like a little gremlin, looking worried. "Like what?"

Ashley perched lightly on the edge of the bed. "I saw the way you changed the subject back in the restaurant when I asked, no, *started* to ask you about the helicopter. And what you said about being a survivor. You weren't just talking about measles and chicken pox. I figured that right out." She took a quick glance at the door to the other room, making sure neither parent had missed her.

Disjointed television sounds drifted through the walls, bits of news stitched together with commercials. Both Olivia and Steven had fallen asleep while watching the nightly news.

Satisfied, Ashley leaned closer to Danny. "I started remembering what you told us about helicopters and police and dogs. I...I know I said I didn't believe you, back at the crater. But now... come on, Danny, tell me what happened to you."

"Oh, that. I thought you meant something different." He looked at her squarely. "People don't like to hear about those things. Nobody likes bad stuff."

"I want to hear anyway."

Now Jack was intrigued enough to join in. "Hey, Danny, all that stuff you said—men with guns—was that real?"

"It was a long time ago." Lowering the blanket

to just beneath his chin, Danny nodded almost imperceptibly. "But yeah, it really happened."

Jack felt his breath catch. "How—when...?"

"Me and my mom. We were boat people."

Boat people?

A memory stirred, but Jack couldn't get a handle on it. Something he'd been taught in class about desperate people fleeing their country in small, leaky boats. He remembered vaguely that the new lands didn't want the refugees and turned them away. But lives explained in the pages of textbooks could seem almost as flat as the paper they were printed on. Until now, boat people hadn't been very real to Jack.

"So what happened?" he asked.

"You don't want to hear this—"

"I do!" Ashley insisted.

Danny's eyes slid from one to the other. He seemed unsure whether to go on.

Finally, hesitantly, he began his story.

"We were trying to get out of Vietnam. See, Vietnamese people didn't like the children of American soldiers, and that's what my mom was. They hated her 'cause she was half white. She wanted to come here to live with Uncle Hien and Aunt Lan."

Ashley bent her knees under her and leaned forward. Jack sat on the edge of his own bed, just as engrossed. "Go on. Tell us," he said.

With his thin fingers plucking the edge of the blanket, Danny continued, "I remember more than anything, my mom trying to get away. She wanted us to have a new life. So we started out, a whole bunch of people crammed into a tiny boat on the South China Sea. We had to sail at night, because the fishermen would chase us. For the reward—you know? We could only escape when the fishing boats were real loaded down with the day's catch, so they couldn't go very fast."

"Did you make it?" Ashley asked.

Danny's face darkened. "The boat capsized. I was pretty little, three years old. I remember the water. It was cold and dark. I—I remember I was crying."

"You were only three? How could you swim?" Jack wondered.

"My mom saved me."

The words hung in the air. For a moment, no one spoke, and Jack wondered at the way Danny could tell the story as if it had happened to a stranger. But this was his story. And it was as cold and dark as the water that had almost claimed him.

"Where was your dad?" Jack finally asked.

"Don't know." Danny shrugged. "Never saw him. I don't even know who he was. But my mom said that was OK, because she never knew her father, either. Anyway, me and my mom got taken into this camp in Hong Kong—"

"That's what you meant by camp," Jack broke in. "When you were talking about your friend Duong Le, I thought it was a summer camp, or Boy Scout—"

"They called it a refugee camp. It was really a prison."

Jack felt a chill creep up his skin. Danny, in prison? He could hardly imagine it. Ashley, too, seemed shaken, but she kept her questions coming, gentle, probing. She, like Jack, wanted all of the story, no matter how bad. For the first time, Jack understood how hard it must have been for Danny to carry this around inside him.

"How long were you in the camp, Danny?" he asked.

"Three years. All that time, the officials tried to make my mother sign papers so we'd get sent back to Vietnam. They said we weren't refugees, we were illegal aliens. But they promised that if we went back, they'd give us immigration visas in six months and then we could leave for Hawaii. My mom knew that was a lie. So she wouldn't sign, even when they got mean with her."

There was no sound in the room, no motion except for the curtains stirring in the open window.

"It wasn't so bad for me. I had my friend Duong Le, the one you remind me of, Jack. He was a lot like you. Not in the way he looked, but other things. Duong Le taught me English.

He learned it from the missionaries. Even though it was awful in the camp, we still had fun together. But it was bad for my mom. I won't tell you what they did to her."

For a moment Danny's voice faltered, but he went on.

"So then, the officials told everyone we'd have to leave pretty soon anyway, because they were going to close the camp. And that part was true. They'd be sending us back to Vietnam then, whether my mother signed or not."

Ashley got off the bed and began to pace at the end of the room. Jack knew his sister well enough to understand what she was thinking. The same thoughts had been pounding through his own mind. They'd been impatient with Danny, tired of his endless talking, angry at his over-confidence, which had led them into so many frightening places. But this kid, this small boy with a big mind, had been through more than either one of them could imagine.

"What happened to Duong Le, Danny?" Ashley asked.

Shaking his head, Danny whispered, "I really don't think you want to know this part."

"Go on. Please! It's OK. You can tell us."

Danny's voice grew lower. "One night it was raining hard. *Real* hard. Duong Le and some other guys cut a hole in the fence. Seventy of us crawled through. We thought the storm would hide us, on the other side, so we could escape. For a while, it did."

Ashley stopped pacing and knelt at the foot of the bed, not missing a single word.

"My mom and I hid in an irrigation ditch, but the sniffer dogs found us. The soldiers shot twelve people that night. My mom and Duong Le—they died."

"They died? You saw your own mother get killed?"

"And Duong Le. Anyway, I don't want to talk about it anymore," Danny said. "I shouldn't have told you such sad things. My aunt Lan said I should never put my pain into another person's heart."

Ashley threw herself the length of the bed and tried to wrap her arms around Danny. "I'm so sorry," she wailed.

Looking embarrassed, Danny wiggled out of Ashley's awkward embrace.

"What for?"

"For the way I got mad when you only talked to Jack and stuff. But I didn't know your friend died. Your friend was like Jack?"

"Uh-huh. He listened to me, just like Jack. When I tried to tell my aunt and uncle about the camp, it made them too sad, so I didn't have anyone to talk to. In a way, it feels good to remember my mom and Duong Le again."

Jack could hardly swallow, because there was such a big lump in his throat. How could this little kid have stood all that? "The most important thing is that you made it, Danny," he told him. "You really are tough."

"Yeah?" Danny smiled at Jack. "You think so?"

Wiping her tears with the palms of her hands, Ashley said, "You're awesome, Danny. But now I'll never be able to sleep."

Jack knew he couldn't, either. Too many awful images were taking shape in his mind. Danny, age six, in an irrigation ditch with his mother and his best friend dead beside him. If Jack fell asleep now, his dreams would be terrifying.

He wanted to move so that his mind would disconnect from those horrifying thoughts. "I have an idea. Let's go out on the observation deck," he suggested. "Just the three of us. We can't see the lava erupting from there, but we could probably see the glow in the sky."

Ashley turned her back while Danny and Jack pulled on their shorts. On tiptoe, the three of them crept out of the room.

With his usual caution, Jack remembered to pocket the key.

The corridors were quiet. "Should we take the elevator?" Ashley whispered.

"Better not. If anyone saw us get off the elevator in the lobby, they'd start asking questions," Jack whispered back. "There's some back stairs. We'll go down that way."

Jack had also remembered to bring along a blanket, but he hadn't folded it, so it hung down behind him. As they quietly descended the steps, Danny picked up the tail of the blanket and carried it like a bridal train, which gave Ashley the giggles.

"Shhhh!" Jack warned.

Without running into anyone, they made it out onto the observation deck, being careful that the door didn't lock shut behind them.

They pushed three chairs close together in a line, then sat with their feet on the edges of the chairs, knees up, arms around knees, and the one blanket covering them like a tent, with just their heads poking out.

"There isn't much glow from the lava," Jack said, "but the moon's pretty. My dad likes to take pictures of the full moon. He does it about every month."

"Why's he keep doing it?" Danny asked.

"He's always hoping for just one perfect picture," Jack answered. His dad was funny that way. Both Jack and Ashley would do a project once—like homework—and that was more than enough. For them it was finished and done with. But his dad kept trying, over and over again, to push the envelope just a little further. To get something more, or make something better, whatever he was after. He hoped Danny's grandfather would be like that. Danny deserved something better. After all he'd been through, Danny deserved perfection.

"This is nice," Ashley said from her seat in the middle, between the two boys. "It's so quiet. Like we're the only ones awake in this whole place. It makes me feel—safe."

"Yeah," Danny agreed. "All the bad stuff from today is over. It's like...we made it."

"Except it's not over."

The voice came out of the shadows, a sound that made Jack's stomach freeze. Whirling around, he searched the darkness until his eyes made out a large shape pressed against the wall. It was tall, heavy, menacing.

"Who—who are you?" Danny stammered.

"You know who I am and why I am here."

"No! I—I need it!" Danny cried. "Go away."

Ashley's head whirled from Danny to the shadows and then back to Danny again. "Danny!" she breathed. "What's happening?"

"It's nothing!" To the shadow, he begged, "Please leave me alone."

"I can't." She moved out of the darkness then, her wild black hair casting moon shadows behind her. Slowly she came toward them, her hand outstretched. In a low voice she said, "You have something that belongs to me."

11

I don't have anything!"
Ashley cried. "I didn't even pick a single ʻōhelo
berry. Danny ate some, but I didn't."

The woman seemed to hesitate. Then she
turned to Jack and asked, "What about you?"

Jack shook his head. At the same time his
mind raced. Had he taken something he shouldn't
have? He couldn't remember anything he might
have done wrong.

Danny stood up, kicked the blanket out of his
way, and moved forward until he was right in
front of the woman. "It's me," he said. "I took it."

"Just a handful of ʻōhelo berries," Ashley bab-
bled. "That's all it was. I know Danny didn't make
an offering to you before he ate them—"

"To me?" the woman asked. She frowned.
Moonlight made her eyes glitter.

"It wasn't the berries," Danny said. Reaching

into his pocket, he pulled out a small package wrapped in white bark cloth. "Is this it? Is it yours?" he asked her, unwrapping the cloth. He held up a piece of dark, polished wood.

"It is mine," she said. "My ʻālana. My offering to Pele."

"But—you're Pele," Ashley cried.

The woman laughed, showing perfect white teeth. "Me? Pele? I'm the night clerk here at the hotel."

In one moment, all of Danny's Vietnamese courtesy seemed to come flooding back onto him. He actually bowed before the woman, saying, "I beg you to forgive me. I shouldn't have taken it. When Jack and Ashley were looking at the nēnē, I found this lying on the path. I should have left it where I found it."

The woman answered just as formally, "I was hiking from Nāhuku—the haole call it Thurston Lava Tube—all the way across Kilauea Iki Crater to Pele's home at Halemaumau. I intended to give her this special piece of kauila wood as an offering. I was focusing on it as I walked, to help concentrate my thoughts and prayers."

There was no sound to the night except the birdcall of a golden plover, far away in the rain forest. Enthralled, Jack and Ashley stared from Danny to the woman. She was no longer dressed in red; she wore a perfectly ordinary jacket with

"Volcano House" embossed over the pocket. Yet she was the image of the Pele they'd seen on the mural in the museum.

She went on, "But my attention wandered. It was wrong of me to lose my concentration, but I happened to see some very juicy 'ōhelo berries. So I stopped to pick them. That must have been where the 'ālana fell out of my pocket. I didn't notice it was gone until I'd almost reached Halemaumau."

Jack was trying to picture where they'd been, where Danny might have found the package, and where the woman had first appeared to them. "So then you came back, and you saw us," he said.

"And started chasing us," Ashley added.

The woman answered, "I knew you children must have my 'ālana. There was no one else around. Why did you run from me?"

Standing as stiff as a steel rod, like a soldier ready to face the firing squad, Danny confessed, "Because I figured the wood belonged to you. And I wanted to keep it."

"Danny!" Ashley glared accusingly at him. "That's stealing!"

"You mean you knew all the time why she was chasing us? What she was after?" Jack demanded.

He answered sheepishly, "Not exactly. Well, maybe. I wasn't totally sure, but...yes, I guess I did."

"You knew! All the way across Kilauea Iki

Crater, all the way through the lava tube," Ashley began. "You knew why she was shouting at us. You knew she wasn't Pele. And I bet you understood what she was saying."

Head lowered, Danny answered, "Not all of it. I can't speak Hawaiian, but I sure understood two of the words she used. *Ku* and *'aihue*. Stop, thief."

Some of it was starting to come clear to Jack, but there were still a lot of unanswered questions. He asked the woman, "You're speaking English now. Why did you yell at us in Hawaiian?"

Gesturing toward Danny, the woman said, "From a distance, I thought he was Native Hawaiian. That's why I kept shouting that my offering belonged at Halemaumau. A Native Hawaiian would have understood how important that was."

Danny said, "I guess I'm not native anything. I don't know where I belong." He sounded tired, and his shoulders drooped.

Now Jack was standing, too. He moved protectively behind Danny and said to the woman, "So you chased us all the way into the lava tube—that's the part I still don't understand. How did you get out of it without anyone seeing you? Is there a secret passage or something?"

Looking puzzled, the woman answered, "I never went into the lava tube."

"Sure you did," Ashley told her. "We heard your footsteps."

"No." As she shook her head, she seemed much too positive for them to doubt. "When you ran to Nāhuku, I stopped chasing you. I had to go to work. My hours here are from five till midnight. I'd left my car at the Kilauea Iki overlook, so I just went back there, got in the car, and drove away."

It was too much to take in. Before Jack could make sense of what she'd just said, the woman spoke to Danny again. "If you knew that kauila wood belonged to me, why did you run away? You seem like a nice boy, with nice friends."

Not even attempting to defend himself, Danny just kept looking down as he answered, "I thought it would bring me good luck. Since I found it here at Pele's home, I figured that would make the luck more powerful. Right now, I need some luck."

The woman reached out to raise his chin with her hand. For a long moment she stared into his eyes, searching them. "I needed it too," she said, "for a personal offering to Pele."

"I'm sorry," he whispered. Danny hung his head again and spoke so softly they had to concentrate to hear him. "In a couple of days I'll be flying to the mainland. I'm going to live with my American grandfather. I never even met him before! What if he doesn't like me? He wouldn't be the first person who didn't like me. I hoped some luck would make things right."

His words hung in the stillness. It was past midnight, too late for birds to call across the night. Even the golden plover had gone to sleep. And they were too far from the erupting volcano to hear any of the powerful sounds of lava jetting out of Puu Oo, each minute adding molten layers from inside the earth to build up a fresh, new surface that would someday flower.

A chilly breeze blew down from Mauna Loa. The moon had climbed higher in the sky. "It is never right to take what belongs to another," the woman murmured. "I can see your need is great, but this 'ālana will not help you. It belongs to Pele."

Danny wrapped the small piece of wood back into the bark cloth and handed it to the woman.

"Thank you," she said. Once more she touched his face with her fingertips. "When I give this to Pele," she told him, "I will ask her to be kind to you." She turned then, and vanished once more into the shadows.

"Where'd she go?" Ashley cried. It had happened so quickly! "She's gone!"

In the moonlight, wetness glistened on Danny's cheeks. For once, he didn't have any words to say.

"We didn't find out her name," Jack said.

"I guess we should have asked her what her real name was," Ashley answered. "Anyway, to me she'll always be Pele."

The significance of what the woman had just told them came crashing down on Jack's head. "She said she never went into the lava tube!"

"Did you believe her?" Danny asked, his voice unsteady.

"Didn't you?"

"Yes. I believed everything she said."

"But that can't be right. We heard her!"

Ashley pulled the blanket tighter around her. "I think I want to go back into the room with Mom and Dad," she murmured. "Right now."

Jack wanted the same thing. He suddenly needed the assurance of his parents' presence. With one last look at the inky shadows, he opened the door and shepherded the younger kids into the hotel.

Very quickly, not saying much, they climbed the stairs and entered their room, with Ashley slipping through the connecting door to their parents' room.

This time, when the lamp was turned off, Danny left it off. Moonlight brightened the room enough that Jack could see him lying perfectly still, staring into the darkness.

Jack fell asleep immediately, but his sleep was troubled. His mind kept echoing the sound of footsteps. They followed him, haunting him.

All night long, he dreamed of the color red.

12

There's gotta be some explanation. I know there is."

Ashley shook her head and said, "Give it up, Jack."

"We're almost ready to land," a pleasant-looking flight attendant told them. Her green eyes turned up at the edges, and her mouth was wreathed in a fine spray of wrinkles that disappeared when she smiled.

Danny took one last sip from his can of ginger ale, then passed it across Ashley and into the flight attendant's hand as she was asking him, "Is this your first time in Jackson Hole?"

Danny nodded. He kept his eyes focused on his lap.

"That's wonderful. I know you'll enjoy it."

Hunched between Jack and Ashley—Steven and Olivia had seats one row behind—Danny looked especially small. They'd been traveling for a long time: Kona coast to Honolulu; Honolulu to San Francisco; San Francisco to Jackson Hole. All of them were tired.

As the flight attendant moved to the next row, Jack leaned across Danny to tell Ashley, "Listen, what we heard in that lava tube didn't come from any spirit. In the real world, everything always has a logical explanation."

"I already told you, it was the goddess Pele," Ashley countered. "If she can turn herself into an old woman, she could make herself invisible."

"No way. Just listen to my new theory. I think I really might have it this time."

Ashley sighed, as though the answer was pretty obvious, and her big brother was stubbornly refusing to admit it. "You've been talking about this for the last three days, Jack. We're swimming in an ocean with Danny, and you're talking about the lava tube. We're all snarfing at the luau, and you're talking about the lava tube. Mom's sleeping in the sun, finally getting her rest, and you wake her up with some lame theory about the mysterious footsteps. We're almost home now, so will you please stop?"

"Just one more. I think I got it this time. It's the roots," Jack announced.

"The roots?"

"Yeah. Remember how the roots hung down

from the ceiling in the lava tube? They had water dripping off them. There must have been a really big puddle on the floor under one of the roots, so then these heavy drops fell down like this—plop, plop, plop. Into the puddle. We were moving toward them, so they sounded louder. It was dark, and we got mixed up and couldn't tell where the plops were coming from. We thought they were footsteps."

Ashley smiled sweetly. "Jack," she said, "you can believe whatever you want. But if you say 'lava tube' one more time, I will personally plop you on your head. And Danny will help. Right, Danny?"

There was no answer. Head bowed, Danny curled his fingers around something so tightly that his knuckles jutted. A look passed between Jack and Ashley.

Both realized that Danny hadn't really spoken, not once, in the past ten minutes.

He'd been chattering away as they'd taken off from Honolulu. He'd talked nonstop when they flew out of the San Francisco airport.

But now, as they neared Jackson Hole, his words had disappeared, like water into sand.

"Hey, Danny," Jack said softly. "You OK?"

"Uh-huh."

"Yeah? That's good. What's in your hand?" Ashley asked.

"My medal. It was my grandpa's. He mailed it to Hawaii when he found out about me. I had it in my pocket."

Gently, as if talking to a baby, Ashley said, "Let me see, OK? Can you open your hand?"

Danny's sweaty fingers uncurled. There, at the bottom of a crumpled ribbon, hung a heart-shaped purple medal ringed in gold. In the center was a gold profile of George Washington.

"Wow," Jack whispered. "That's a Purple Heart. Your grandpa was a hero. That's really awesome, Danny."

"I know. He must have been really, really brave. Except...."

"Except what?" Ashley asked.

"Except, that's the only part I know about him. He was wounded, so he got a Purple Heart. But I don't know what he's like inside. I don't know anything."

"You'll find out all that," Jack assured him.

Swallowing, Danny added, "But—I—I don't know if he'll like me."

"He will," Ashley promised. "I know he will. You don't even need an 'ālana for that. Just yourself."

Danny looked at her. "But what if he doesn't?"

"Then you'll still have us," Jack told him fiercely. It surprised him how strongly he meant it.

Suddenly, he realized how much he wanted

that grandfather Danny was about to meet to appreciate his new grandson. What if Danny's grandfather got impatient, just as Jack and Ashley had? What if he really didn't care for Danny? After all, the man hadn't known Danny existed until a few weeks before. What if he considered it nothing more than performing his duty to take care of Danny, the same as serving in the armed forces? The thought hit Jack hard that the rest of Danny's life was waiting right below them, right now, in the Jackson Hole airport.

"Please return all seat backs and tray tables to the upright and locked position," the flight attendant instructed. "We are now making our final descent into Jackson Hole."

Jack touched Danny's hand in a gesture of support. The Landons would go back to the world they'd always had, but Danny was going to enter a whole new one. Again. The way he'd done so many times already in his short life.

As the plane made its approach, lining up with the runway, sun burst through the small airplane windows and blinded them with a blaze of light. Danny sat quietly clutching his medal, oblivious to the majestic Grand Teton peaks that loomed right outside. Ashley, too, seemed lost in thought. The three of them stayed silent as the plane dropped; they didn't move until it bumped down on the runway of Jackson Hole airport.

"Ready, kids?" Olivia asked. "Here we are."

"No, I want to be last. Let everyone else get off first," Danny begged.

"All right, Danny," Steven told him. "If that's what you want. Olivia and I will walk out with you."

"Can I have Jack take me?"

"Sure," Jack said.

"And Ashley, too?"

Ashley nodded. "You bet."

While Olivia and Steven gathered the last of the carry-ons, Jack led Danny down the steps and onto the tarmac, because the Jackson Hole airport was too small to have a jetway. Ashley reached to take one of Danny's hands, and Jack grabbed the other. The hands were cold and clammy. Danny's face had become almost expressionless.

Step by step, the three of them approached the glass doors to the lobby. Twenty more feet, and they'd be there.

At that moment the doors slid open, and out stepped a burly man with a Chicago Bulls baseball cap snugged down on his head.

He walked slowly, one hand gripping the knob of a cane, the other clutching a smaller version of the red baseball cap.

"Sir," a security guard called out. "You'll have to wait inside for the passengers to join you."

"I'm sorry, mister, but you see that boy? That's

my grandson." And then he called out, "Danny! Danny—I've been waiting for you!"

"Grandpa?"

Slowly, Danny pulled his hands free.

Steven and Olivia held back Ashley and Jack. "Let him go," they whispered. "We'll wait here."

With a slight smile, the security guard stood aside to let the man hobble forward.

"Danny—I'm so glad you're here," the man said. Each step looked painful, but he seemed determined to walk the whole way out to the plane.

"That's OK, Grandpa," Danny called out, breaking away from the Landons. "You stay right there. I'll come to you."

As the two of them came together, the man gently set the red cap on Danny's head.

"Chicago Bulls are my favorite team," Danny said.

"Really? Well, how about that. They're mine, too. We'll watch lots of games together. Just you and me."

Slowly they walked, grandfather and grandson, into the airport terminal.

Danny led the way.

AFTERWORD

You, the reader, have just finished an exciting mystery. Let me tell you of another, here at Hawaii Volcanoes National Park. Not long ago, a volunteer field biologist found a wild nēnē family. They were probably taking their two goslings to the grassy fields nearby. We guided them instead into an open-topped pen, where we hoped they would become part of an experiment. Since so many goslings don't survive through the first year, we're trying hard to discover how we can help them.

This nēnē family had plenty of food and water. But two days later, after a bit of rain, we found the bigger of the two goslings wet, very cold, and lying on its side unable to walk. When I put it in my car with the heater blasting, the little gosling seemed to perk up a bit.

At the research center, we set up a heat lamp over a box, turned out the lights, and banished everyone to keep the noise down.

Later, in the quiet gloom, I tried feeding it. It wouldn't, or couldn't, eat. Although it was up and walking, if it didn't eat its chances of surviving were not good.

Somewhat desperate, I ran up to the park's education center where I borrowed a mounted, stuffed nēnē.

As soon as the gosling saw it, it peeped in recognition. I peeped back. Crouched on the floor to stay hidden, I tilted the decoy nēnē so that its bill was in the box. With my other hand, I waved a leaf near the decoy's bill and made peeping noises.

The gosling tried to nibble, but the leaf was tough and wouldn't tear. With no free hands and not wanting to remove the decoy nēnē from the gosling's sight, I nibbled the leaf with my teeth and returned it to the box. This time the gosling took a small bite!

The volunteers spent many hours feeding the gosling, and eventually managed to get it eating on its own.

When it seemed strong enough, we took it back to the pen. There we found its family.

As soon as the female nēnē heard her gosling peeping, she ran toward it, and the reunited family walked away together.

But three weeks later, when I visited the pen, a bit of fluff caught my eye. It was the gosling, dead in the short grass. What had gone wrong? There were no bite marks, no other signs of predation. I felt frustrated and confused.

At least with predators, we know what we're fighting, as difficult as the battle may be. In mysterious cases like this one, we don't really understand what we're up against. But we'll keep studying and experimenting, hoping to one day solve the problem of why nēnē goslings have such difficulty surviving.

Finding solutions to problems plaguing our wildlife and wild lands takes the work and will of many dedicated volunteers, plus trained staff members and wildlife biologists like me. You, the visitor, can help too. Keep wildlife wild— don't feed animals in the national parks. Plants and rocks are tempting collectibles, but they're also part of some creature's habitat and part of each park's unique beauty. Please be a good caretaker in our national parks. With all the wonderful life forms they hold, they're a part of your heritage.

Darcy Hu
Wildlife Biologist
Hawaii Volcanoes National Park

ABOUT THE AUTHORS

An award-winning mystery writer and an award-winning science writer—who are also mother and daughter—are working together on the National Parks Mysteries!

Alane (Lanie) Ferguson's first mystery, *Show Me the Evidence,* won the Edgar Award, given by the Mystery Writers of America.

Gloria Skurzynski won the American Institute of Physics Science Writing Award.

Lanie lives in Durango, Colorado. Gloria lives in Salt Lake City, Utah. To work together on a novel, they connect by phone, fax, modem, and e-mail and "often forget which one of us wrote a particular line."

PARK DATA

STATE: Hawaii, on the Big Island of Hawaii   **ESTABLISHED:** 1916

AREA: 229,177 acres. UNESCO World Heritage site and International Biosphere Reserve

CLIMATE: Warm and breezy on coast, cool and often wet at Kilauea, nightly freezing & occasional snow high on Mauna Loa

NATURAL FEATURES: Two of the world's most active volcanoes, Kilauea and Mauna Loa, jagged cliffs, dense forest, lava trails

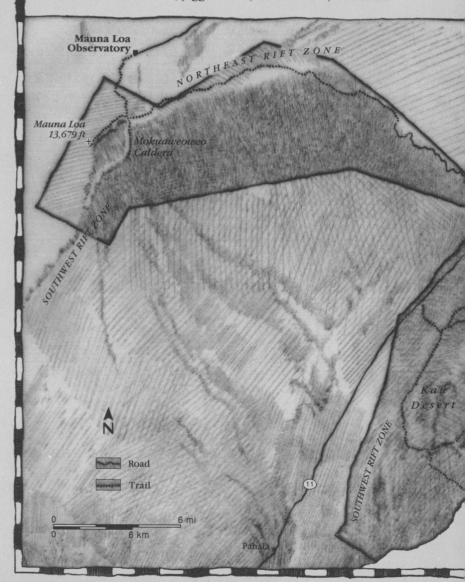

Mauna Loa
Observatory

NORTHEAST RIFT ZONE

Mauna Loa
13,679 ft

Mokuaweoweo
Caldera

SOUTHWEST RIFT ZONE

Kau
Desert

N

Road

Trail

SOUTHWEST RIFT ZONE

0   6 mi
0   6 km

11

Pahala